The Jumping Off Place
by
Carol Christian West

Matchstick Literary
1-888-306-8885
orders@matchliterary.com

The Jumping Off Place

Dorrie and Cliff were the first arrivals at the oil company that Cliff managed from his wheelchair.

Unlike her usual high-energy self, she sat Monday morning donuts down on her desk. Then she sat down in her chair, deep in thought.

"Cliff, did you ever have a premonition that something bad was going to happen, something that you couldn't stop?"

"Sure, Dorrie, when my son and I had just started the company and were operating in the red and still learning the ropes, I came in the morning wondering if we had made a huge mistake and were going to lose the company."

"Did you have a bad feeling that day before the truck bed fell on your legs?" Worry creased Dorrie's forehead.

"You mean about my becoming paralyzed and ending up in a wheelchair?"

"Yes."

"Well, no, I didn't, Dorrie. Now that you mention it; it's a wonder I didn't. Maybe just certain people have that ability?" Dorrie was a very perceptive person usually.

"Mom always says women can sense things better than men. I think it depends on the man. Some are just as sensitive as women. I know my father is."

He didn't mind Dorrie's questions. They could talk about anything. She was the daughter he and Margaret had never had and the sunlight in his days. Usually.

"Well, Cliff, I woke up this morning with a bad feeling, and I still can't shake it. You know me. I usually sing or read you a joke if I'm down,"

"You sure do, Dorrie."

A commotion interrupted from outside. Cliff's eyes moved to the window Dorrie had her back to.

The expression on Cliff's face changed immediately and what Dorrie saw there was fear, major fear, turning his face white!

Chapter 1

VANTAGE POINT

He had stopped hearing Galveston's sermon. He was staring at the back of her head once more. Two rows behind her here in church he could do it without anyone knowing. What was he feeling for her? He loved the shape of her head, the honey-colored hair swept high but not too tight so that wisps of it lay over the collar of her dress, the flowered one that brought out the color of her blue eyes. He admired her inner beauty, too, the kind way she reached forward to help Mrs. Murrell remove her raincoat. He wanted happiness for her, though, and he was not sure he would be able to give her that.

Nearby a man stared at another woman but wished he could strangle her. It was a wonder she didn't feel his hate. He felt she posed a tremendous problem. He wanted to be free of it. If she had turned and looked at him, she wouldn't have understood his hatred. It wasn't normal after all. He certainly wasn't hearing the minister's words on brotherly love. Far from it. He was already revising a plan, one that would accomplish his goal.

In still another seat, a woman noticed a man's slender hand as it lay on the top of the pew in front of her. His hand look like an artist's. He wasn't one that she knew of, but she did realize the very caring way he did his daily work. Everyone in Sweetwater did. Some girl would be very lucky to catch his eye one day. He'd be a very sensitive partner.

Galveston Hobb's rather benign sermon on brotherly love ended this Sunday in the Sweetwater Pentecostal Church. It had covered the required points; it just wasn't rousing. Galveston sighed inwardly. It wasn't too difficult from his vantage point to know everyone hadn't been paying attention.

Chapter 2

WAKE UP SWEETWATER

At the close of his sermon, Galveston moved to the next item on the program.

"Folks, I'd like to ask Dorrie Humber to step up to the pulpit. She has asked to speak to you all on a matter of concern to everyone. I'm sure you will give her your attention."

A dark-haired woman with serious brown eyes and slightly bent posture quickly moved to the pulpit from the front row where her husband, Ted, and their two boys, Bryce and Dan, sat.

"Pastor Hobbs, friends, and members of this community and church. Something has come to my attention that I felt should not wait for the next town meeting. I have worried for a long time about the new phosphate mining company that has come to Sweetwater and how it affects our town."

At these words people glanced aside at one another but said nothing. Galveston tapped his fingers on the pulpit chair and peered up at the ceiling lights. Were Fulton and Adam here this morning? He let his eyes drop to the back seats where they sometimes sat. Oh, yes, both. Oh boy, he thought, both president and vice president of the company.

Dorrie had noted the two men who were attending. Also there were some who were employed by the mines present, she was sure.

"When it was approved that the company come here by the state and local landowners, I was worried about how it would affect the health of our town. I am not a scientist or in the medical profession, but I don't have to be to report what I found at the rear of my father's farm yesterday."

At this point, some whispering stopped. A kid who dropped a hymnbook midway back for a little attention suddenly got lots of stern looks.

Somebody's stomach grumbled from hunger in the choir.

Abby Fuller, Dorrie's mother, picked that moment to whisper loudly to Ollie, Dorrie's sister, "Will you go get my sweater from the car? I'm cold."

Ollie went. No objection.

"I will be quick to say that many jobs have become available to people through the mining company. They kept that promise. It does seem to be bringing more people to our community from other places. Our town has grown."

Fulton and Adam looked at each other and nodded largely with satisfaction.

Ollie re-entered the church with the sweater.

Dorrie continue. "I walked yesterday to the very back of my dad's strawberry farm. I was devastated to find a number of dead birds and small animals near the gypsum mounds that have been piled up from the mining. They died obviously from the breathing the fumes around the holes in the tops of these mounds or drinking the water from these holes. If they died, what will the mining do to our drinking water? Will it make us sick or kill us? That's what I wanted to bring to you this morning. I submit we should require an investigation into this and have our present drinking water tested immediately!"

Dorrie moved with straight back, determined expression, and lifted eyebrows back to her seat. Her mouth held a no-nonsense line.

Immediate murmuring began as people digested what she had said.

"Oh, no!" and "I told you I had smelled fumes" and "This is awful; what are we going to do?"

Galveston heard a lot from where he sat. He rose from his chair, looking into worried faces in every pew.

"Is there anyone who would like to add to what Dorrie has said?

Please stand where you are and wait to be recognized."

The first woman who stood looked towards the member to her right.

"I agree with Dorrie. Water samples should be taken by non-employees of the company, probably the health and sanitation department, and be tested tomorrow."

Ollie, Dorrie's sister, sitting in the row back of Dorrie felt very proud. She was afraid to make a speech like Dorrie did, but she could raise her hand.

When Rev. Hobbs called on her, she said, "I agree with Dorrie, too."

Chapter 3

OLLIE'S RETURN

Ollie Sullivan had returned to Sweetwater, her town of origin, after her husband, Carl, had died of a heart attack. Her first husband, James, had died of a heart attack, too. Some people just said they were both too old for her.

Her sister, Dorrie had called her when she'd realized Ollie's depression was lasting too long and told her she should just come home and they could spend time together like they had when they were growing up. She said Ollie just needed friends.

That was enough said to Ollie. She loved Dorrie dearly and had not wanted to say how much she missed Dorrie when she and James had married and moved away.

Dorrie was all the things Ollie wished she was. Quick-thinking, outgoing, smart in business matters, creative… Whenever Ollie had questions when they were growing up, she'd gone to her sister for answers. Dorrie didn't make Ollie feel dumb for asking them like Mama did.

When Ollie had come back to Sweetwater, she hardly knew what to make of all the changes in her hometown since the mining company had come. Allgreen Mining Company had brought with it a whole lot of new people, looking for jobs, opportunities, new adventures, and the new life starts. Ollie wondered how she was going to fit in now. Mama had said Ollie could live with her and Papa and help them out. So Ollie had parked her trailer in her parents' yard and there she'd stayed. That had been two years ago.

Chapter 4

SOME OF ALL

After the controversial speech Dorrie had made at church that morning, Abby was reminiscing with Billy about a town meeting they had all three attended.

It had been in May of 1962 before the mining company came to Sweetwater. It was no secret that economics of the time had welcomed a new company and a lot of jobs. Farming and fishing had been suffering. Any money they made from tobacco farming came and went quickly. A lot of the crab and fish had disappeared. They didn't have all the answers on that.

Billy reminded Abby, "Pollution further up the river from manufacturing firms contributed to that. And we switched to strawberry farming to try a different way of making a living."

"Even when everybody laughed at us for doing it. They didn't laugh long. We've done alright, Billy. I've always been proud you didn't buckle under the fun they made."

"Well, they were just the people who didn't know what to try different."

"And one of the fishermen said,'Might as well try mining'. "I remember that. Abby rubbed the furrow between her eyes.

"You remember that doctor from across the river said folks who wondered what mining would do to the area should fly along over the waterfront beach homes along the Pamlico."

"Yeah, and the guy stood up in the back of the room and said, "Well, if they rode around the area they'd see farm houses falling down because the farmers had no money to prop them back up.""

"And then, a lot of the farmers said Amen to that."

Abby closed her eyes for a minute. "Weren't there almost three hundred there?'

"Right, but some of those were from countries around who'd benefit from the mining jobs that would be offered."

"Was it the doctor who argued that they ought to put in the contract that an equal amount of land mining should be required for a river mining allowed?'

"Just one of the landowners. Because you remember one fisherman hollered out, "That'll make the landowners rich. That's what they're after.' "

"O.K.," Abby remembered. "That's when one of the landowners said, 'We just want our share."

"And the officers of the company said there'd be 'some for all."

"So, is Dorrie right or wrong?"

"I reckon a water test will shed light on that. Course, I'd have thought they were already doing that, as a precaution. What will all the environmental folks raising questions."

"Allgreen Mining is here...for good or bad."

"That's right, Abby."

Chapter 5

ADAM KINCAID PHILYAW

As a child Adam Kincaid Philyaw heard his father say more than once that the government had ceased to be the help for the poor and tired – that it now protected the wealthy and the powerful, and he wasn't going to help them. He'd fight them single-handed if he had to. So the child would go in the backyard, put his toy pistol in its holster, climb a tree and drop water bombs onto his unsuspecting victims, the cat and the dog.

He saw his mother act a helpless, unintelligent dependent she thought his father wanted, and his father berate her for being a spendthrift. He couldn't see how they could so totally not know each other and be married. And so he told his teachers he had a learning disability (he thought) and they didn't require as much of him as he otherwise could have produced. Meanwhile he found amusement in trying to beat the doctors at the tests they gave him. He saved his bigger thinking power for the important stuff – how he'd keep people afraid of him and how he could punish those who dared stand up to him.

When he joined lockstep with Fulton in college, he knew they were an unbeatable team. He would rather have mined diamonds in Africa. That sounded so exciting. But he had invited a lonely geology professor out for drinks one night and after the man was practically in a stupor, he had volunteered his theory that phosphate was up and coming and mineable in the states. It was also capable of making him a fortune.

He knew Fulton had cheated the same way on the college finals, and he knew great minds did work alike and could work together. He'd just have to watch his back and Fulton, but then he'd always done that and still could.

Chapter 6

FULTON T. OSGREEN

Fulton T. Osgreen had never brooked opposition well. When he was little and his mother gave him orange juice he detested, he poured it on her indoor gardenia when she wasn't looking. When the flower died, she never knew why. When his father advised him that to go out and play he had to eat his spinach first, he snuck the spinach and put it behind the boxwoods. They were so rotund with years, no one could see the base of them anyway. When the babysitter said he had to go to sleep, he appropriated flashlights from his father's tool supply to read his comics. He knew her boyfriends visited her at his house without his parents' knowledge and used that information to get what he wanted, extra candy, unlimited popcorn and bubble gum, even special toys she had to buy with her allowance.

He never cared how he got his way as long as he did. Needless to say, his mother never developed a green thumb and his father appeared inept because he could never find a flashlight.

In school he collected secret information on the other students and thereby convinced them to write his reports. It didn't matter that he didn't have lots of friends; he had major practice getting his way. His classmates made fun of his name, anyway. They said it sounded like a piece of lawn equipment.

That was part history of his becoming one of the two top officers of the phosphate mining company. And he wasn't about to take any opposition now.

Dorrie Humber represented the most serious obstacle he had met in years. She was thoroughly antagonistic to the phosphate mining in her hometown. She didn't have to know a lot about mining. She felt it was bad for the water and the animals and birds. And if it was bad for them, how could it be good for people? So she mounted her soapbox any chance she got…in the dinner, in the drugstore, and in the church.

Chapter 7

GALVESTON

Galveston Hobbs was the preacher of the Sweetwater Pentecostal Church. His father, who had named him said it was a fitting name for a preacher.

"Preachers don't have it easy. They need big names to live up to." When he told his wife what his daddy had said, she raised her eyebrows.

"Well, honey, they see all these beautiful women they can only talk to, not touch."

"Is that a fact?' she said.

At that point, Galveston thought he should refer to his dad.

"That's what he always said, honey."

"Mmm," she said.

When he was small, Galveston loved to watch his father shine his shoes for the Sunday service. His father would counsel his little boy just like he was going to become a preacher. "You have to talk to the people on the back seat. If you do that, everyone will hear you. You also have to have something worth saying. Not just preaching because you love the sound of your own voice."

When Galveston actually grew up and became a preacher, his father had more wise words: "Be honest about everything, your ability, the church offering and the ladies in the church choir." And so he had. It had served him well because a former preacher in the Freewill Baptist Church believed in a little too much free will with one of the sopranos in the choir, and he was banished by church vote.

It was like his Daddy had said. You could only look not touch the lovely ladies in the church. Abigal was no exception. He admired the back of her head and all the black hair piled up when she played the piano in church. Abby was not beautiful, but she had such spirit. She could not play the piano and sit still.

His Daddy talked like he knew about everything like he knew about car engines. And his dad liked church music.

Ruby, Galveston's wife, was a fine preacher's wife. She'd served on the school board before he was called as a minister, and he'd met her there, speaking on one of her personal soapboxes, the right of women to serve on committees and be chairpersons of them, whether church or school committees. She was passionate, too. He admired that about her.

If they ever had a boy, they'd name him Houston. They'd decided that, or a name after a Bible prophet. Galveston's Dad was no longer living, but they knew he would like their thinking. "Give them big shoes to grow into." He'd always said that about raising children.

Chapter 8

FLYING AWAY

Abby Fuller sat down to the crackled finish on the old mahogany piano in the front of the Sweetwater Pentecostal Church. It didn't matter about the five cracks in its sound board. She could still play it and make good music. She didn't need sheet music to play. It was all in her head. She could hear a song once and then play it. She believed this was a gift from God. Nothing else she did make her so happy.

No one had ever questioned her pianist position in the church. They were downright glad she had the gift. After all there weren't but thirty-five of them in all. And they existed two hundred feet from the Free Will Baptist Church of Sweetwater who had to sing acapella for the present. The members of Abby's church were sure this was the sign they were right in their beliefs, but Free Will said no, they had a leading soprano voice in Leona Jenkins. That much was so.

"I'll Fly Away" was what Abby was playing and what she was doing from all her cares. She could do that playing the piano the way many people played the radio, except this way she was in control of what she heard. None of that bass beat popular stuff. She could play hymns like the strong masterful sounds of "There is a Fountain Filled with Blood" that would purely transport her away or "Come Thou Fount of Every

Blessing" that would remind her of the first time she saw Billy. She remembered looking at Billy's eyes when he was listening to her play, and she saw them closed, and his face looked simply angelic. She'd known she was in love. She'd be able to lead him. He had passion for the church and it's teaching. Nothing was so majestic as "The Church's One Foundation" from one end of the piano to the other. She loved the great hymns like "Lead On, Oh King Eternal." It was so spirit-filling to play it. She could make the glass in the windows purely shake with the strength of her playing. When the basses in the choir heard her play, they sang all the louder. It was very moving.

Chapter 9

"TOUGH SOLDIERS"

Ollie and her father were listening to a country album while Abby was over practicing piano at the church. They had had to close the windows of that side of the house in order to hear. Abby played from one end of the keyboard to the other by ear and never softly, either. She told Ollie or anybody else who asked that the Bible said "Make a joyful noise unto the Lord" so why use the soft pedal, ever? Ollie had just kept quiet and thought, well, it must have been put there for some reason.

Ollie's favorite country artist was Ronnie Milsap. He was blind and still achieved. Look what he can do she told herself. The story of Helen Keller when her mother had read it to her as a child had kind of overwhelmed her. Unbelievable what she accomplished. Her Papa had said he understood how she felt…why she could relate better to Ronnie.

"You know, Papa, Dorrie used to say "Tough Soldiers, Ollie!" when she was trying to get me to do something."

"Really, girl. You want to be a soldier?"

"No, Papa. Just think like one. I remember some words Dorrie said, a poem…to get me going when I didn't feel like it."

"You do, Ollie? This is great! I never heard about this between you and your sister. Tell me the words."

"It went like... "Tough Soldiers, they all have a song.

"Tough Soldiers, they can get along.

"Tough Soldiers, they can save the day.

"Tough Soldiers, they can make a way."

"I never heard it; Ollie, I like the words. Does it have a tune that goes with it?

"Well, I remember, the one she sang it to. She used it with me when I was trying to learn something new like tying my shoes, or buttoning my clothes, or spelling words.

"Oh, I see. Pretty smart."

"She is Papa. I wish I was smart."

"You're thinkin' about important things, Ollie, right now. That's smart."

"Really, Papa?"

Chapter 10

OLLIE'S REFLECTION

Ollie sat on the little padded bench in front her dressing table mirror in her trailer bedroom. Why had she never seen her mother with makeup on? She reckoned that was part of her mother's religious beliefs. Sometimes in the Old Testament it said women were not to "decorate" themselves. Mama wore only simple cotton dresses. She wore no bright colors, no lipstick. Since she had been back home, Ollie had not worn makeup either. She did this out of respect for Mama, but it did not help her state of mind. She was already prone to depression. She did not argue with her mother. If she did not agree with something her mother said, she simply looked at her lap or out the window, or did a chore. She was afraid her eyes would give her away.

Her eyes. They were faded blue, not dark and flashing or smart like her sister, Dorrie's. More than anything she wished she was smart and looked like Dorrie. Dorrie looked like Mama. Ollie was told she favored Aunt Marion, her father's pretty sister who lived in Roanoke, Virginia. She'd never even had a conversation with the woman. She'd just seen two pictures of her, one on a train. Going somewhere. She had long, curly honey-colored blonde hair and blue eyes. She would have traded her figure like Aunt Marion's in a minute for brains like Dorrie's. Aunt

Marion didn't have a reputation for smart either. She was said to have married the first man who asked her. Ollie was afraid she'd done that, too, He was the first "safe" man who'd asked her. A lot older, but he'd been kind. Ollie was told she stood out in a crowd. She didn't want to stand out in a crowd. She wanted to hide if she couldn't be smart. School had been hard for her. Even though Papa helped her, she finally dropped out in eighth grade. At that point she wasn't passing any tests. She had just started helping Papa around the farm and Mama around the house until one day when she was 17, she came home and told them Mr. James Olsen had told her he loved her and would she marry him? They would live in Newport News. He was taking a job at the shipyard at Norfolk. It seemed Mama had looked relieved. Papa had tried to make her wait. He kept asking her did she love him? Mama had never told her love was necessary to getting married, though. Mama had thought James was nice enough and told Papa she thought he'd be good to Ollie. After all, did he want Ollie to keep slippin' around meeting Luke Gentry after dark and get in trouble?...

Ollie looked down from the mirror to open her pocketbook. Inside the zipper pocket she found it, a lipstick Dorrie had given her. She pulled the top off the tube and then, looking back to the mirror, she drew a red line on her upper and lower lips. She moved her lips together and noticed in that moment her eyes looked bluer.

Abby had never cut her own hair. Ollie thought that was also ordered by the church. She didn't braid it; she didn't wear decorative combs, berets, or ribbons. Just a bun. That was allowed. Ollie shook her head from side to side. She couldn't believe it. God even made the birds with colors, so why couldn't women use colored ribbons or berets in their hair? Looks at the parrots in the jungle.

Ollie reached for the brush and swept her long, curly hair up on first one side, then the other. She pushed the blue combs in place she had brought when she moved back but hadn't worn. They had been down in the bottom drawer in a bag with combs of every color. Hidden away.

Ollie puzzled over other questions. Why did the church say that women should be subject to their husbands? Well, Mama wasn't subject to anybody. Mama rarely even said "Yes, Billy" about anything. Papa had to win his points for sure. Actually Mama told Papa what to do. Or else he checked with her first. It was easier to live in this house if you didn't argue with Mama. Not exactly happier, just easier.

How did Dorrie get by having her own set of beliefs? Could it have to do with Dorrie being so smart? Mama really respected smart. Another thing, Dorrie always figured out Mama's needs before Mama even said what they were. So Mama appreciated that. Such as Dorrie hearing Mama say she was going to sew. Dorrie would offer to help her before she even asked.

But Dorrie was always at work and Ollie was at home where Mama could tell her what to do. Dorrie always announced stuff right before she did it, and she didn't say "May I? either. 'Like when Dorrie cut her hair. She cut it and said she had to have it short for work. She didn't have time to dry it before going. So if things were going to change, Ollie was going to have to change the way she did things. Maybe not giving Mama time to think about it first by having done it already.

She could still remember Dorrie coming in the door at Mama's in her first pantsuit. Pantsuits were not allowed by the church. Men and women were supposed to dress differently. So that meant women couldn't wear pants or jeans. Dorrie had just said her legs were getting cold at work and that was the end of it.

What was the difference between how Mama acted with her and how she acted with Dorrie? She had never understood. She knew she wasn't as smart as Dorrie by a long shot. She accepted that. Maybe Mama didn't and thought she could change that by changing Ollie somehow.

After all, she was already starting on her housekeeping habits. Ollie hadmissed some stuff out of her trailer. She was going to have to ask her mother about it. She sure didn't look forward to that. But she had this hunch it went along with not tracking mud in and always drying the dishes. That was a pure waste of time to Ollie. That time you spent drying the dishes you could be hearing a new bird sing or seeing him, or planting something that would grow. Dorrie didn't believe in drying dishes either. Look at all the books out there that you could read while you were wasting time drying dishes. Dorrie said that.

They could drain dry.

Chapter 11

OLLIE'S KEEPSAKES

Ollie had lots of things in her trailer she couldn't get rid of. She hadn't really tried to, but she knew she couldn't throw them away. Her mother had told her she could keep it neater if she threw away 2/3 of it. But Ollie felt it was like throwing away pieces of her life.

So she kept the stuffed animals her first husband gave her during their courtship... little teddy bears, kittens, puppies she had hoped to give their first child when it came. It didn't.

She kept the tiny glass creatures her second husband gave her during their two-year marriage. She had hoped for a daughter to pass these to. That didn't happen either.

Smaller dresses she kept in case she lost weight. Books she'd been given on death and dying and grief she put on the first shelf in her bookcase. She hadn't really read them yet. She'd tried, but they made her too sad. A book called "Sunshine" she kept on her coffee table. It had made her happy and she read from it often, a page at a time.

She didn't really know why Mama made such a big deal about her keeping her things. How would Mama feel if somebody told her she should get rid of some of all that piano music she'd collected? She didn't play from it that much. She played mostly by ear. Ollie knew Mama wouldn't care to be told that. But then she, Ollie, would sure never tell Mama to get rid of things she had. She just knew they meant something or Mama just liked them.

One therapist had told Ollie she had filled her trailer with substitutes for friends who'd moved and husbands she'd lost through death. He told her not to worry about it unless she started talking to her dresses and asked them which one wanted to go out with her today!

Chapter 12

THE SHOWDOWN

She'd said "Mama," three times at the door of Mama's room. Mama had not answered. She was sitting in the rocking chair by the window with her Bible in her lap and her eyes closed.

"Yes, Ollie, is what you want so important you have to interrupt my Bible study time?"

Her eyebrows went first up and then settled down into a frown.

"Well, I thought you just might be dozing, Mama. Your eyes were closed."

"Ollie, what else can you do with your eyes shut?" The frown hadn't gone anywhere.

"Pray, Mama." Ollie replied dutifully. She noticed her Mama's smile return with that answer, but by then she almost forgot what she had come to ask. Oh yes.

"Mama, what happened to the stuffed animals that were in my trailer on my bed?"

Ollie, I was in there the other day to return some of your finished laundry. You'd forgotten to take it to your house. I saw them on your bed. I thought Ollie's too old for these.

Don't you think your bed looks so much better without them? I do."

"Mama, what did you do with them? James gave me those. My husband."

"I put them in a bag to take to Goodwill, of course. James is dead, Ollie. He won't know"

"Where are they? You had no right. They're mine!"

"Oh, Ollie, honey, we'll get you some nice pillows for your bed. Aren't you embarrassed for anyone to see them?"

"No! Mama! I want them back. You just don't want your friends to see them, do you?"

"Believe me, girl, I wouldn't take them in there. The way you keep everything. You are a real packrat!"

"It's my trailer, Mama! I want them! You're ashamed of me!"

Ollie felt her face and neck getting red.

Her mother noticed that. "They're in the pantry! I'm not ashamed of you except when you talk to me like that. You need to mind how you talk to me!"

Chapter 13

THE JUMPING OFF PLACE

The rain made gray, foggy soup of the visible space on the road. It was almost mesmerizing. But as he drove, he had to remain alert. This was the only time he had to think about what he was going to do, to review his plan. Certainly, he was thinking if he'd stayed home back when he married, at least in the same town, he and his father would have a much closer relationship now. His father had always been a good man. It had not been hard to love him. But if there hadn't been all that time in between, it would make what he had to do a lot easier. Or harder, depending.

He was returning home to Sweetwater. He was totally broke. He had told them about Angela leaving, but he hadn't mentioned he was penniless. He would have to humble himself a little at first, ask for help if it weren't forthcoming. He understood the house his Dad had rented next door to a couple was empty now. Just maybe.

When he left to marry Angela, she changed him in all the ways he'd been a good man before. She was so ambitious it was contagious. Now he was no longer content with the bringing up he'd had, getting by, growing what they ate, having enough clothes, just adequate housing. He was in the realm of superlatives. He wanted the best, the most of everything. That's why his plan had to happen soon or he'd lose his mind.

How far would he be forced to go to right himself, to get on his feet again? He wouldn't be satisfied with getting along. He wouldn't even be satisfied to keep living here. Who was he kidding? He had two sisters. He wasn't an only child. They would figure in the will. He had to get his hands on that too, to see what it said. He probably already knew. His father would not let those girls do without. Maybe he could offer to handle things, money, especially. His being the oldest and all. And if that didn't work.

Well, he'd have to see.

At he looks around at the wet landscape, the water collecting in the ditches beside the road from the rain, he was reminded of the infernal mosquitos in this jumping-off place. They had been enough to make him want to leave Sweetwater. Sweetwater, indeed. All the water he saw in the swelling creeks was black, nothing he'd ever wanted to swim in, or catch fish from to eat. He hadn't wanted any fish since he left here. Now there was a mining company in Sweetwater. It had come here four years ago. He understood the waters were changing. They were drying up.

At least the phosphate mining company was offering jobs to people. That was something he'd have to follow up on, probably. There were precious few other employers in this hometown.

"Welcome Home," the big Nagle sign said. It was an advertisement for a restaurant but Donald took it to mean him, the somewhat prodigal son returning home. He sat taller in the seat.

Chapter 14

DONALD'S PLAN

Donald sat in the house next door to his father's and become totally miserable when he looked at more bills that has arrived from Raleigh. How in thunder would he pay them? The alimony check he'd just sent Angela left him "broker than an old mule's back."

Of course, having to have a new well dug hadn't helped. He looked out the window and what he saw gave him a bitter taste in his mouth. The same scrubby pines in the distance, desolate, ugly fields next, and dry parched grass in his own yard. He despised this landscape.

He had come back here for only one reason and ultimately his wife left him because he had come back. They had spent so freely when he'd married her and moved to Raleigh (where they both thought they'd be happy) he'd lost their house. He had come back here to get in Papa's good graces again, to see if he would will the family strawberry farm to him when he died. He smiled to himself. When Papa had found out he'd lost the house, he had offered the one he owned next door to his and "Mama's".

It was so hard for him to call his stepmother, "Mama." She was nothing like his real mother had been. Lenora had been beautiful, blond, and graceful but had left him and Papa when he was eight years old, saying she would be back for him later. She had died in a foreign country with no way to come back and get her boy. He knew that had been so. Two years later when Papa had married Abby Fuller, he figured it was more for her piano playing and good cooking.

Chapter 15

FINANCIAL PLANNING

Donald once again had gone over his bills. He finally stuck them back in the desk drawer and slammed it shut, causing a chip of wood to fall to the floor. There was no way around it. He was no genius at figures. But it didn't take one to know that his back-up plan couldn't be avoided. He had to convince Papa that he was getting older and needed someone, specifically Donald, to handle the finances and the farm. He remembered that Papa had admitted to him that his memory wasn't as good as it used to be. And that he misplaced things sometimes, bills, sometimes even money. Hey, maybe he could help Papa to misplace some of that money into his palm. He surely needed it.

He started whistling to himself. That was some good thinking he had just done. Sometimes a man just needed some peace and quiet. Now when would be the best time to approach Papa? For one thing, when Mama wasn't around. Maybe in the truck riding somewhere. By themselves. He reached over and turned on the old brown plastic radio Mama had brought over when he had moved back into the house. She had said it was to keep him from getting too lonesome.

He looked out the window. This landscape was beginning to get to him. How much sadder, poorer could it get?

"Take this message to my mother It will fill her heart with joy.

Tell her that I've met my Savior. God has saved her wandering boy."

Hank Williams on the radio brought Donald back. How did this radio get on a gospel station? He surely wouldn't have put it there? Oh yes, he knew. It had to be Abby. She's been in here again. She was trying to convert him. It would never happen. He went to church because his father went. He could hardly bear it. Any of it. The music the whiny voices, nasal, his real mother used to call them. She had said all they needed was a good antihistamine.

She had had a solo soprano voice.

"Glory to God! He remembered me."

"What good is gold and silver too? If your heart is not true"

He switched it over to a rock station. And turned up the volume. Took his ruler and started tapping out the rhythm on the desk. Hard. Then what he saw out the front window made him change the station back to the gospel music. Abby was coming up the front walk.

When he heard her knock, he was at the screen quickly. She was smiling broadly.

"Donald, I see you like the music. That's great! I knew it'd grow on you. After all you're Daddy's boy."

Donald smiled back at her.

Chapter 16

DONALD GETS A JOB

It didn't take long for Donald to discover that, like it or not, he was going to have to get a job somewhere. Looking around Sweetwater, he also knew that unless he planned to put a lot of miles on the car every day, there was only one place to work and that was Allgreen Phosphate Mining.

He knew he couldn't afford to even put gas in the car on a regular basis thanks to Angela's extravagant spending. All his cards were at maximum level.

Maybe his father's name would carry some weight. He was beginning to sound like the prodigal son. But no, he hadn't been the wasteful one. That had been Angela. Mostly. But he had chosen her, hadn't her? How could he not have seen how she was? He was blind, as he always had been with a pretty woman. So it still came back to him. He was so tired of that. He had to come crawling back home to a place he detested that was hardly on any map.

Would his having worked in Raleigh for a big real estate firm help him out? Hard to say. He'd been a fair salesman, but he hadn't filled any executive position. Well, he was hardly going to get one here. And he was not going to get into the actual mining. That would be slave work. So what did that leave? He was about to find out. He was sitting in the outer office of the executives here. His 10:00 a.m appointment was with Adam Philyaw. Impressive sounding name. The door was opening and a small-built, perfect-postured man with a welcoming smile, approached him. Not the size man he'd expected but he had to admit the man's whole demeanor said self-confidence and success from short, blond, perfectly waved hair, small cleft dimple in his chin to his little hands but firm handshake. He probably handled public relations, too.

"Come right into my office. Have a seat. Your father must be Billy Fuller. Billy's a fine fellow. I admire his venturing out into strawberry farming. Took guts."

"Thanks, Mr. Philyaw. I reckon Papa's a hard worker, too. That never hurt anyone in the farming business.'

"Right you are, Donald. What kind of job are you looking for? What kind of work did you do in Raleigh?"

(How about one question at a time, thought Donald. What you really want to know is why am I back? Assuming you knew I left.)

"I was in real estate, but after a while there were as many realtors as lawyers in that area so I thought this might be an up and coming company.

I wanted to come and talk to you all about a future with you."

"Well, Donald, we have an accountant position open. The fellow who held that position for a short period lied to me on the application and in the interview. He said he had four years' experience in accounting. That God we found him out before he made off with the money."

"Well, I'm certainly no accountant, Mr. Philyaw. But I can't afford to be picky. My ex-wife has left me high and dry. You know, big spender."

(He had not planned to volunteer all that.) I don't mind taking anything to start with. You have to crawl before you can walk. Dad said that."

"Well, Donald, all I have is maintenance technician supervisor opening. You would supervise the janitorial work. Would you be interested in that?"

"Sure, I'd be glad of it, Mr. Philyaw. I've got to better my status financially before I can be choosy.'

"You've got it then Donald. Could you come in for tomorrow for training?"

"Sure, the sooner, the better."

Philyaw extended his hand. "Glad to have you on board, son"

As Donald went back out to his car, he wondered. How could this, a man half his size call him son? And how many ways tomorrow could they teach him how to clean bathrooms or mop a floor?

Chapter 17

"I WOULDN'T BE ANYWHERE ELSE"

The job at Allgreen Phosphate he could hardly bear. They'd given him the title of maintenance supervisor only to make it go down better; he knew that. Fancy name for a janitor. But it at least gave him an inroad with the biggest employer in town.

Papa had come in one morning when he was cussing the overalls he had to wear on the job.

"Son, they look fine on you. How are you gonna wear them when you're lookin' after the farm one day, if you can't abide them now?'

"Oh, they are ok, Papa. Just not my favorite thing. They're such trouble when you use the john."

"Son, look there at the front. You've got a snap on an opening there to take care of that!"

Donald felt so stupid. How could he have forgotten that? Many a time Papa had stepped to the woods when he had the mule and plow in the field.

"Don't you remember going to the fields when I farmed tobacco?"

"Sure, Papa,." Thank goodness he wouldn't have to look after the farm when he got hold of it. He'd sell it to the first person with the money. Probably the phosphate people. It backed up to the Phosphate Company land anyway. That was how Dorrie had made her discovery that the fertilizer processing wasn't any good for small animals. She'd found dead ones near the gypsum mounds where they had tried to drink water. Even dead birds that had been killed by drinking the water. She figured if it weren't good for animals, it surely couldn't be good for people. She was probably right. She was smart. But not as smart as he was. He knew he'd be out of his jumping-off place as soon as he could work things out.

"I sure am glad you pointed that out. I can't believe I forgot that! Thanks. It'll sure save me gobs of time at work."

"Sure, son. I reckon it's been a long time since you wore overalls. Do you have any idea how good it is for me to have you home? It really helps me that you are here. Your Mama, too. Family is so important!"

(If you only knew. Papa, I'm sure glad you're not as smart as I am.)

His father took a step over and puts his left arm around Donald to embraced him.

Donald wiped at his eyes as if they were wet.

He said with emotion, "You know I wouldn't be anywhere else, Dad."

Chapter 18

DONALD'S REVERIE

They could be so much consolation to each other, if she'd allow it, his half-sister. He hadn't had a chance to ask her about it alone. He would have to arrange that. They could meet sometime, maybe have dinner. She had lost a husband; he had lost a wife. Donald had to admit to himself, though, that sometimes she said things that made no sense. Those little things she said that didn't seem intelligent. He remembered the day they'd been in the back yard.

"Papa, just look at that purple wisteria hanging from the trees. That shows even God has second thoughts, doesn't he?"

"What do you mean, girl?" Papa had been thinking about Donald's new job.

"Well, the tree didn't have any blooms, so God made the wisteria decorate the tree."

"That's igno—' Donald started to say, but thought better of it. "That's a nice thought, Dorrie."

"What did you say, girl? I'm sorry my mind was somewhere else."

"She just said that the…" Donald started.

"Nobody has to talk for me, Donald!"

Whew! I better keep my mouth shut! Thought Donald.

His mind drifted. Or, that time she had said that God could make her smarter anytime he wanted to. Where did she get that? She said if He was powerful enough to look after the world, He could. Donald wanted to ask her why hadn't he done it already. What reason could God give her for not having done it? It would just make her madder that a wet hen. No he surely didn't want to do that. It was right with him if Ollie had the looks in the family. It was also just fine with him that he was by far the smartest person in this family. Although he did wonder about Abby sometimes. He would probably have to look out for her. She worried him a little.

Like that day recently she had walked into her bedroom when Donald thought she was out and caught Donald looking for some of Papa's papers and his will.

"Can I help you find something, Donald?"

She had scared him so badly.

"Oh Mama, I er…er… Was just looking for one of Papa's ties I might barrow. For work."

"I didn't know you ever wore ties to work, Donald. I thought just overalls."

"Did I say work? I meant church! Land, I don't know where my mind was!"

Good thinking on your feet, he told himself. She has seemed pleased he was thinking about the church. Mercy, how could anyone not think about it in this house.?

Chapter 19

LIP READING

Abby watched Donald. His lips were moving. She thought that was strange, but then she remembered she talked to herself, too, when she was planning things like supper or the music for Sunday church service. What was Donald planning? She thought she never watched his father for long periods like this and certainly not to wonder what he was planning. Did men do that?

Well, he was deep into it. He hadn't heard her come in the door.

"Donald, a penny for your thoughts.'

"You mean my prayers."

He'd seen her come in, alright.

"Oh well," she said. "Admirable. You even beat me to it. Donald, this early in the morning.."

"One can't pray too much, Mother, can one? (You better; your ship is sinking fast, he thought to himself.)

"Absolutely not." Abby beamed to think Donald was finally subscribing to some of their teaching. But there was a slight nagging in the back of her mind.

When had she ever seen Donald praying before? Then she felt bad for thinking it.

"Don't' dare let me interrupt you. You go right ahead." And she was off to her day.

When she left he went back to his hand-wringing and gnashing of teeth.

"How do people stay here?" he muttered. "This place without the mosquitoes would have me packing an overnight bag, never to return."

No wonder they pray so much, he thought. There's nothing else to do.

You had to go 25 miles to a theater to see a movie. No one, certainly not their church believed in television. He remembered that was one of the reasons he had had no problem leaving.

Even the bar in the nearest town was so poor, they could never afford to hire entertainment.

Well, he bet Ollie would appreciate the brotherly gesture of offering to take her to a movie. Sometime later today he would do that.

Chapter 20

THE MAGIC OF THE PULPIT

Galveston felt cold but the weather wasn't cold. Neither was his house. He got up from his dining table where he usually studied and walked to the hall to retrieve his brown cardigan from one of the coat hooks by the front door. Slipping it on he then shivered his way to the kitchen to stand in front of the wood stove. He poured another cup of black coffee from the percolator sitting on the iron top. What was the matter with him? As he stood rubbing his hands and feeling the warmth, he wondered if he was getting older and his circulation might be the problem. He spied the red of the coals through the hole on the lid, and they hypnotized him, and he finally felt the heat penetrate his bones.

Back at the table, he rearranged the cushion about to slip from the ladder back chair and settled back down to ponder the service when Dorrie had raised the question of the water sample. He'd felt very inept at handling things. He'd felt this knawing inside to have Fulton come up to the pulpit to address the congregation. But he hadn't said a word. It was the confrontation issue. He knew it. He didn't want to stir things up. He didn't want to anger Fulton. So what could he have done? He could have done the obvious. He could have asked anyone who spoke to come up to the pulpit so everyone could hear. This was an important issue for the community. So why was it so hard for him to handle things? Take charge, a voice in his head said. If he had, it would have made it easier on him. Fulton would have had to look at Dorrie and the congregation when he spoke. Then Fulton couldn't have addressed everything to him, the minister, and not talked to Dorrie, the person he wanted to avoid. Why didn't he think of this solution yesterday when it happened? Fulton got by with murder, actually. Fulton should have given Dorrie the respect of looking her in the eye when he spoke.

He, Galveston, had grown uncomfortable with the way things were headed. Dorrie Humber had asked a simple, important question quite directly and had deserved to have his help. Fulton, with his college education and powerful position in the community, had help the trump card over a woman who worked hard and was honest as the day was long.

Take a deep breath or two, he said to himself. More oxygen to the brain. He lifted his shoulders until they touched the back of the chair, inhaled and held it, expelled it.

Twice. Three. Four times.

Miriam, the church secretary had warned him, "If you don't mind my saying so, Galveston, you can't take Dorrie's side all the time, so quickly, even if you think she's right. People would think you were playing favorites. Believe me I've seen that before. It can make battlefields in the church. Members get jealous of the attention the preacher pays. It's one of their human traits."

There was another thing he was wrestling with. He remembered Fulton coming to his office one day. It must have been very hard for the man to admit, "Preacher, I've done a lot of bad things in my life."

"There's really no way to make amends for some of them. Some of the people I've wronged are dead. My father used to tell me to go to church or meet him in the woodshed after church. It made me hate church. Now I want to come because I make that decision myself, and I like you.

"Thank you, Fulton. You mind telling me what you like about me?

"Well, it's like you don't browbeat people into doing things; you don't lay guilttrips on them. You inspire them."

So he had figured Fulton might be a lonely man and realized he needed God and church at this point in his life. If he strong-armed this issue, he might run Fulton away.

Something his father had said to him when he knew he wanted to be a minister came back. He had told him Theodore Roosevelt's famous words about the presidency...

"The presidency is a bully pulpit."

Here he was with a pulpit and not using it to the best advantage. Well, that was going to change. Dorrie had spoken from the pulpit before, undaunted. Fulton or Adam could do the same when they were questioned. He suspected they had been present to smooth the waters, anyway.

"You must have just made a big decision, G. You've got that determined look on your face. And look how far you've rocked in that chair?" His wife giggled as she stood with her hands on the hips in the doorway.

"You were so intent you didn't see me come to the door."

"A big decision alright, honey... I just hope I can follow through."

"Do you want a sounding board?"

"Yes, Ruby, if I tell you about it I can't back out as easily. Sit right here and let me explain it.'

The pleasure of being included always showed on her face.

Chapter 21

TRIP TO THE MINE OFFICE

Ollie and Papa had become very concerned one night at supper. Ted, Bryce, and Dan had come over to eat supper at Mama's invitation. Dorrie was coming as soon as she got off work. Mama made wonderful white sausage gravy and biscuits, and they could rarely resist that menu.

Ollie noticed the red rash on the boys' skin first. They weren't scratching it, but there it was.

"Ted, have you seen the rash on Bryce and Dan? Where'd they get that? What is it?"

Ted and Abby and Billy all looked around at once at the boys' skin.

"Good heavens! I see it, too. You boys been in the poison ivy?" "Abby got a scowl on her face like she could.

"Grandma, we've been at work; you know that! We haven't had time to go hunting!"

"She's right, though. Where'd that come from, fellas?" Looks of consternation now appeared on Ted and Billy's faces.

"I don't know," Bryce looked down at his arms. "Probably a shower will take care of it.'

Dan fingered his face. "It feels a little like sunburn."

He looked at his brother. "You know they did tell us to go home and take a shower every day, and we haven't been doing that exactly.'

"We don't have an inside shower. The shower's outside." Ted now spoke up.

"Maybe we ought to go to the mine office and ask if anyone else has broken out in rash," Ollie puzzled aloud.

"We can do that for Dorrie; she's working, "Billy agreed.

The next morning Ollie and Billy knocked on the door of the mining office. The man who invited them in wasn't particularly friendly.

"I'm Randall and I'm in charge when Mr. Philyaw and Mr. Osgood aren't here, so address your questions to me. "He showed them onto his office.

"Wow, a lot of mining dust is in here, too." Ollie commented as she brushed his desk with her hand. "It has a funny smell about it."

"Excuse me, if we can get to your questions, I have other things to do."

"Oh, O.K. My father, here, and I have two boys, Bryce and Dan, from our family that have been working here during the summer and have rashes now on their skin from it. Have you had other employee's skin to break out?"

"No, nothing of the sort. They've been no reports of... Ah.. choo!! Randall reached for a handkerchief.

" My sister, Dorrie, their mother. She'd want me to ask. Sheconcerned about them working here, but their father saw the money as helpful, so he allowed it."

"That's right. Is there a lunchroom where they all eat?" Billy joined the conservation. "Seems like that would be better to get away from all this dust." He looked around, too. "Oh, and how about showers they could use?"

"Well, Mr B.... we aren't running a posh hotel here, so no. there aren't showers and a separate dining room. Take those up with the bosses if you like. Now, if we're done here, I'll show you all out."

He stood up, massages his sinuses, reached in his desk drawer, and pulled out the Sinutab pills, sitting them beside his bottle of water.

"Well, if you say we're through, we'll go." Ollie sniffed and stood up.

She was actually taller that Billy remembered.

"Also we remember how we got in, no need." Ollie waved Randall off.

"We, that was not helpful, was it?" She asked her Dad when they were out of hearing.

But Billy was thinking how Ollie had stood up to Randall the way Dorrie would. He'd never seen her do that before.

Chapter 22

SINKHOLES AND
WATER SAMPLES

First, she raised her hand, then thought better and stood up.

Galveston knew it was Dorrie before he looked to see whom the hand was attached to. They usually sat further up toward the front.

"Preacher?"

"Yes, Dorie."

"I just wanted to ask a representative, I reckon Mr. Osgreen who is here, what'd been done on the water matter since we talked the other Sunday. I called the company Thursday but couldn't get anyone who knew."

"Fulton, could you address Dorrie's question from the pulpit so everyone can hear?"

Good, it was all first names when someone complained. Maybe that would keep things from getting too serious or at least keep them civilized. Galveston knew he wasn't good at confrontation. No better now than when Tommy Popperville popped him in the third grade when he wouldn't fight.

Fulton's voice brought him back from the playground reverie.

"If Mrs. Humber will walk down and look at the sinkholes near the poverty line between her father's farm and Allgreen Mining she'll see we have covered them."

Where was Adam this morning? Thought Galveston. He was much the better of the two to deal with what Fulton was talking about to Dorrie.

"They've been covered with dome screens to keep the birds and animals out. That's good – but the fumes are still there. And I've found some dead birds on our property, evidently they got sick from the fumes."

"Can Mrs. Humber prove that, Rev. Hobbs?"

Uh-oh, thought Galveston. We are back to last names.

"No, but my main question about the town's drinking water.

Is it safe? Has it been tested?"

Galveston was painfully aware not one word had been addressed to Dorrie.

One woman stood and spoke. "Well, I'm boiling all our drinking water 'til we know."

Her neighbor also stood to contribute. "We're just drinking soft drinks or juice or milk, no tea or coffee until we know."

"Oh, brother," one man muttered, "I've got to have my coffee."

His comment got a lot of nodding heads and oh yeses.

"Just boil your water."

"Boiling may not make it safe." Dorrie was standing again. "Steam rises from the sinkholes."

"We're doing the best we can." Fulton said finally and sat down.

"Could we take the water sample to them?" Dorrie wasn't sitting.

"It has to be tested here, Preacher." Fulton crossed his arms over his chest as if to close the matter.

There was some murmuring.

"Alright folks, I'm sure Fulton and Adam will let us know as soon as they have information. Everything's being done that can be done. We'll call this meeting to a close. Will you bow for our closing prayer?"

As soon as he raised his head, Galveston noticed Fulton was once again one of the first to leave.

Chapter 23

ADAM AND FULTON

Adam was poised in his office chair reflecting on what Fulton had told him about the second incident at the church. He noticed his drumming a pencil on his desk had finally gotten on his nerves and left a mark. Hmm. He didn't allow other people to sit in his office and mutilate his desk. Well, that was his prerogative, after all. It was his desk.

What had happened at the church didn't bode good for the business. He knew that. Dorrie had never been positive about anything about the mining operation. Adam had gotten across to some people that it would mean more jobs for a dying community, that Sweetwater could look for growth and profit, even, after a while. But Fulton have been attending the church for almost a year. He said he was doing this with the idea of the people getting to know him, but Adam recognized that Fulton's loyalty to the local population was beginning to usurp his loyalty to him. He remembered Fulton making sounds about keeping the church updated regarding any possible health hazards.

Adam hadn't planned to update anybody about anything. That was giving out information that could come back to hurt you in the end. Adam knew there was money in mining. One didn't mess with making money. That was jeopardizing your future. He had never felt there was any question with Fulton's loyalty to their operation. But yesterday a question peaked in his mind. After lunch Fulton had walked in to stand at the front of Adam's desk. Usually he just had a seat until Adam looked up from his desk work.

"Adam, when do you think we'll get the results of the water testing? I didn't have any for Dorrie or the community when she asked the second time in church."

"So"

"Well, you know, she's asking questions. The people see her as their spokesperson, their advocate."

"And"

"If we don't have any answers, soon, I'll bet she'll call for a county healthy inspection at least."

"She'll probably do it anyway."

"But maybe not if we had an answer to her question. She'd think we were listening. We need to be forthcoming if there is a problem."

"We don't know the answer to that, and we won't even the tests come in."

"But they're finding dead animals and birds at the gypsum mounds. Why is that?"

"I don't know. Maybe a concentration at something at the mounds."

"You know it's bound to be."

"So what?! Do you want to kill our operation? Our money-making proposition?"

"Do you think Dorrie's going to sit and wait for no answers?"

"Maybe not."

"So what are we going to do, Adam?"

"I don't know, Fulton. Let me think of it."

"You now a solution that I don't know?"

"I'm not sure."

"We'll advise me." And Fulton had left. Just like that.

He did know one thing. He was not going to let anything or anybody stand in the way of making fortunes. He knew that was going to happen in Sweetwater. For him and Fulton. If Fulton would keep his mouth shut. And Dorrie.

Chapter 24

COFFEE BREAK

Dorrie smothered a giggle when she looked over to see jelly on her boss, Cliff Turner's chin.

"O.K., I heard you snicker. Was is it? Just because an old man is in a wheelchair doesn't mean he can't hear!" Cliff looked around at her, his brown eyes raised sternly over his reading glasses, but his mouth was smiling.

Dorrie pointed.

"There's evidence on your chin. Be sure to take Margaret two of these." Cliff's wife loved jelly donuts. "Well, that's excellent counsel, but how can I be dignified enough to run this business if you're gonna let me drool?" Cliff laughed out loud and reached for a paper napkin.

He loved to tease Dorrie. She was the child he and Margaret had never had and his right arm in this business. Her keen mind anticipated needs before they arose. When the falling truck bed had taken his legs, God had supplied Dorrie. It was true he'd provided help for her boys when their father hadn't. He liked doing it. He loved her like a daughter and she returned his faith in her.

"Boy, they were good. Worth the calories. Thanks for bringing them." Cliff reached for his coffee mug.

"Twice as good if you share a good thing. The Lord invented two good things with coffee and donuts, didn't he?" Dorrie questioned.

"What day did he do that?" Cliff mused.

"Had to be Monday, I think. Here let me get us a refill." Dorrie reached his mug and turned to the percolator on the hotplate on her desk. After filling his she poured herself some in her favorite mug. No. 1 Mom, it said.

"It's about time for Briggs, I better save him a cup."

Chapter 25

THE GOOD SAMARITAN

Bill Briggs, the older, tanker truck driver for the Esso Oil Distributor, climbed carefully down from the seat in his truck. He walked around it and reached down to pull off the cap to the underground tank of the service station. He pulled the nozzle of the gas hose from truck and pushed it down into the tank, making sure it connected. He checked that the gas flow dial was on zero, pushed it forward to "On" and watched it engage. Satisfied about its flow, he learned back against his truck to wait for the fill-up. He fingered the small paperback dictionary he had in his shirt pocket. Tonight, when they were finished with supper, he would help his granddaughter with her...

A loud, jarring noise ahead of the truck shook him from his thoughts! He ran around the truck to see what? Straight ahead his eyes riveted upon a car that had just crashed into a telephone pole. As he watched in shock, the driver keeled over in the front seat. Briggs' mind left his watch and his work.

"Oh my God. what?" He almost fell as he ran back toward the car, to the driver's side. Through the open window he saw the man clutching his chest.

"Hold it, fella. I'll go get you some help! I don't know CPR!" Briggs started to move away.

"No, no, don't go, please. Don't leave me! Get the pill! The man was pointing to the glove compartment.

So Briggs opened the door and tried to prop the man up to breathe better. He yanked the small glove compartment door open, got the brown bottle out, the lid off and saw the man swallow the pill.

But by then it was too late. The gas that had been running into the underground tank had overflowed, escaping down the hill into the oil company office and exploding the gas stove there...

Briggs stumbled back to the pump to turn it off, but there was dread in his heart, and pain that suddenly seized his whole chest. He collapsed beside his truck with no one to run and help him.

Chapter 26

SMALL TOWN CRIME

When people of Sweetwater heard the horrific explosion, they ran onto the sidewalks from everywhere. They dropped their silverware and ran out of the Canna Lily Cafe. Men bolted from Sim's Barber Shop with shaving cream on their faces. Shoppers at Perry's Grocery left their carts on any aisle and raced out of the store. The drugstore, the hardware store, the Peace Methodist Church all emptied. Everyone looked in the same direction toward the oil company down at the end of the Main Street. Mouths fell open at the dreadful flames and black gusting smoke filling the air. No one noticed the man in the car pull away from the telephone pole.

When the firemen found the bodies, there were two, charred beyond physical recognition, but in an amazing physical posture. One victim's arms had been locked under the other's trying to drag the body from the fire. The firemen, all volunteers, had known who the victims were before the investigation into the fire. One was Cliff Turner the owner of the Shell Oil Company and in a wheelchair. The other was Dorrie Mae Humber, his secretary, accountant, and general girl Friday.

The firemen also knew, before the Sweetwater Weekly News printed it, that a gasoline tank had overflowed on an incline above the office. It had run down the sidewalk, gathering momentum until it reached the door, flowed underneath it, and ignited the stove ten feet away.

Chapter 27

ABBY'S REACTION

After Chester McHenry, the undertaker, had left, Abby had gone from the angry, assertive question about why did God take her smartest, brightest girl to a giving up sort of posture.

"Well, if there was a fire this bad, what could she do; what could we do?" She was told the firemen had clothes burned off them trying to save her.

"This is a bad horrible, bad dream, Billy. I'm going to sleep now. When I wake up, you'll tell me this didn't happen."

That part sounded more like her business-like attitude about things. This nightmare would never go away, though. He watched as she lay down on the daybed in the sitting room. He trudged across the vinyl floor he had dutifully laid over the solid wood one to please Abby. It popped under his feet. He bent down to cover her with the yellow, brown, and orange afghan from the end of the bed. He tucked it over her shoulders, and stood over her for a moment.

Then he heard the deep, heart-wrenching sobs and "No, No, ... No, , ,No, ….. Dear God, No. It can't be. Help me, God."

That went on until she was exhausted and closed her eyes.

"It happened, Abby; I'm so sorry." He said it as if it were his fault. He limped back to his rocking chair to nurse his grief but didn't leave her and reached over at one point to pull the straying black and gray hair from her bun up on top of the collar of her dress. Her body curled on its side into a fetal ball under the cover.

An hour later, after mostly shaking his head and wiping the endless flood of tears from his swollen eyes on his sleeves, he noticed Abby was asleep. He rose slowly from the rocker, his bones cracking, and went to look for Ollie. It occurred to him that she might have heard the awful question that Abby had asked God about taking her smartest, brightest daughter.

Chapter 28

OLLIE'S GRIEF

Billy thought he knew where he'd find Ollie. And she was, in Dorrie's old bedroom. He leaned his round body quietly against the door frame and didn't speak. Ollie was sitting on the bed, looking out the window. She held against her body two old cloth dolls, one hers, one Dorries's Finally she groaned aloud and she lowered her body to the hook rug beside the bed. Still clutching the dolls to her chest, she sat beside the bed and lay her cheek against the silk patchwork-square quilt that covered the bed. She had her eyes closed and began to sob Dorrie's name over and over. The quilt held Dorrie's name in the center and had been made by Abby for Dorrie when she was twelve.

Billy had admired the brilliant colors and his wife's talent in making the quilt.

"Abby, that is a prize of a quilt!" He'd said.

"I didn't make it for the county fair, Billy!"

"I know; it's for Dorrie. She will love it. Have you thought about making one for Ollie, too?"

"Billy, do you have any idea how much work that represents? Ollie wouldn't appreciate all that work. I'll make Ollie a simple one. She wouldn't take care of that."

And that was the end of that discussion. As smart as his wife was, why didn't she know Ollie would see she was treated differently?

Billy walked over to the bed, sat down by Ollie and stroked her hair.

"Oh, Papa, she was so good, it should have been me that died. I'm not good... for anything."

"Hush, girl, you know how much comfort you give me. You make me happy." And Billy remembered the "Sunshine" song he had sung to her in the front porch swing when she was little.

"Really, Papa, are you sure? I wish... I wish I"

"What, girl?"

"I wish I could make Mama happy."

"Don't worry about that, Ollie. She's pretty hard to please. I know that. And Billy rolled his eyes at Ollie.

"It's not often I can even do it."

Ollie dried her face then and took Papa's hand to get up. She sat the dolls down side by side against the bed pillows.

"Papa, what are we gonna do?"

"We'll have to find our way, girl." And he squeezed Ollie's hand, "A day at the time."

"Thank God I have you, sweet one. You and I understand one another."

"Come on, let's go on the let's go on the kitchen. That sounded like someone came in the back door."

Chapter 29

DONALD HEARS

It was Donald at the door.

"I came as soon as I heard about the fire. Tell me she's alright. Tell me she's o.k.. It's not true."

"No, it's true, son. Chester was just here." Billy rubbed his long-sleeved shirt cuff across his eyes.

Donald hung his head. "Oh, dear God. Not Dorrie." But he knew when he looked at his father's face.

"Where is Mama? How's she taking this?"

"She's lying down. She said when she wakes up she'll know it's a … a bad dream."

"Oh, God, son. Oh, God." Billy broke down and grabbed the table for support.

He sobbed aloud as he leaned, his eyes scrunched up and tears plainly fell on the tabletop. "What did she ever do to deserve this? She's always been so good to everybody."

"Nothing, Papa," Ollie wrapped her arms around Billy's waist and laid her head against his back.

"O.K. you two are going to wake Mama." Donald tiptoed over to the parlor door and closed it.

"You know, people sleep sometimes when they're trying to deny something,"

Donald tried to explain.

"Deny something?" Billy sounded puzzled.

"Well, like that Dorrie's dead.'

"Oh, …"

Donald noticed that Ollie was staring at him. He looked back to his father.

Billy rubbed his eyes and pushed away from the table.

Donald stood with them in a circle for a moment, no one saying anything, then he broached the inevitable subject.

"Have you all discussed arrangements yet with Mr. McHenry?"

"No, son. It's just happened!'

Donald saw Ollie fold her arms around herself and look at him disbelievingly.

"I'm sorry, Pop. You're right. It's just somebody's got to do it soon."

"He's coming back at 3:00."

"I doubt she'll be able to do this, you know." Donald gestured toward the other room.

"I could stand in for her with you."

"Well, I'm not going to leave her out of it, unless she says so. You know Abby."

"At least I'm not going to tell her he's coming."

"I think Mama would want to." Ollie raised her hands, palm up.

"Even if it's the hardest thing she ever…" "She couldn't finish. Her fist was over her mouth. Her other hand clutched her waist.

"Pop, I'm gonna grab a sandwich, alright?" Donald was pulling open the refrigerator door.

"Help yourself, son. The ham is in there from Sunday. Ollie, you, too."

"I'm not hungry, Papa."

"Me neither, Ollie," Billy left to go in the other room where Abby slept.

As he pulled his chair up to the bed, Ollie heard him speak.

"I wish I could bear all the pain, Abby."

Donald downed the last of the ham sandwich and thought, *Wow Mama, you're a good cook.* I'm gonna miss that when I leave here. Of course, then I'll be able to buy it made… the very best. As he got into his car, he reached in his pocket and pulled out the last of Mama's brownies from Sunday. "Mmmm, Mmmm," he murmured as he backed out of the drive.

"No one who looks as good as Ollie should be my sister." He said aloud as he pulled away.

Chapter 30

PLAN FOR THE FUNERAL

Mama had the freshly ironed handkerchief with the pansies on it, folding and unfolding it on her lap. It had been in a box of three Dorrie had given her. Just in case, Ollie got the whole box of Kleenex from the kitchen and placed it by the loveseat Mama sat on.

Papa let Mr. McHenry in by the front door. Ollie knew he'd never looked sadder.

He came and stood in front of Abby.

"Abby, Billie," he took Mama's right hand in his. "I can't tell you how awful this terrible thing has made us all feel. Everybody loved your Dorrie."

Mama closed he eyes and nodded her head up and down. Papa sat down beside her on the love seat and circled her back with his arm.

"Yes, they did, Chester, no question about it." Papa's voice was soft.

The phone rang. Ollie moved numbly to the next room to get it.

"Yes, Miss Leona it surely was. Thank you. She surely was." Ollie's voice broke.

"You do? That's very nice of you to offer. I'll tell her. She and Papa are talking to Mr. McHenry right now. O.K., bye." Ollie wondered if she was doing this alright. Dorrie was usually the one.

The doorbell rang. When she answered it, Mrs. McGillicutty and Mrs. Reynolds from down the street had brought fried chicken and some potato salad. Mrs. Murrell, the postmistress drove up in her car. She let herself in with a chocolate cake.

"Oh, Abby, we're so sorry, oh sweetheart." Cora McGillicutty walked behind Mama and leaned down to hold her cheek next to Abby's Her arms went around Mama's neck. Cora and Mama were both crying now. Cora had no daughters and had always loved Abby's as her own.

"Oh, Abby," Clara Murrell whispered and shook her head in disbelief.

Ollie took the cake to the kitchen and sat it down next to the silk jonquils on the oilcloth – covered table. Papa brought the meat platter first and then the potato salad to the table. Ollie felt sick when she looked at the food. She didn't even want to smell it, and it was all food she liked.

When she returned to the living room, the ladies had left. Mr. McHenry was saying the casket would have to be closed. Ollie looked at Mama and felt a hard band around her chest. It was getting hard to breathe in this room. If they didn't finish soon, she'd have to go outside. The windows weren't open. Maybe that'd help. She tried to open one then remembered the locks. When she finally got one open, Mama complained.

"Close that Ollie, we'll get dust rising from the front road."

Ollie sighed and closed the window. When she turned to leave the room, Mama spoke again.

"Put any meat in the refrigerator, Ollie." Now Mama wouldn't have anybody but her to give orders to. Dorrie was gone. As soon as she thought it, she covered her mouth and ran down the hall to the bathroom.

She turned the spigot on full blast and closed the door. She fell down onto the floor and groaned into her hands and apologized "I'm so sorry for thinking that, Dorrie. Please forgive me." She finally could breathe better after she cried.

When she came back into the room, Mr. McHenry was asking what should they put on Dorrie.

"Her red dress. Red was her favorite color." That was an easy answer for Ollie.

Mr. McHenry raised his eyebrows and looked at Mama.

"No, red wouldn't do. It would have to be the navy one with the white collar. Ollie, go to her house and get the blue one and the circle pin with the colored stones that stood for the family. Wait, you can't drive. Billy take her and get the dress."

Ollie cringed inside. It wasn't her fault she couldn't drive. Mama wouldn't let her try the test. Papa said give it time.

"Come on, sweet, I need your help." Papa put his arm around Ollie's shoulders and they walked together out the front door to his truck. As they rode to Dorrie's, Ollie told Papa about the call from Leona, the soprano from the other church. Mama hadn't let her interrupt the conversation.

"She offered to sing, Papa, anything Mama would like. You know Mama can't play for Dorrie's funeral. It wouldn't even be right."

"You're exactly right, Ollie, I'll tell her, although she may not like it.'

Billy thought this was one-time Abby would have to accept help.

Chapter 31

TED'S LOSS

Ted sat at the funeral wedged between Bryce and Dan, his and Dorrie's boys. He hoped he could stay like this for a while. He looked around at people crying and felt guilty because he couldn't. He could not really think what it was going to be like. Without Dorrie. Clara and Cora sitting back three rows to his left had already given him looks he thought meant "Why in the world aren't you completely beside yourself?"

His Daddy had always told him it was weak for men to cry, usually after he had taken his belt to him. So this was the biggest test. To see if he would cry. He wouldn't care who saw him crying now. Why was his brain so confused?

Dorrie had always been the strong person in their family. The boys always asked her questions about school work. He knew she was smarter than he was. He didn't mind that even if some of his friends teased him saying, "Don't let her be the boss with all those brains she's got." It was true she had never acted dumb or helpless like some women did just to attract a man. He had kind of admired that about her.

If something got broken about the car or the house, though, she knew to call him, and she had even told the boys to watch how he fixed everything. She had told them to learn how to build things and do repairs like he did them, not to just learn fishing or hunting from him.

He had appreciated her determined look and confident smile in the tenth grade. She wasn't the beauty queen sort his friends liked. She knew what she wanted and told him it was him for the time being. She had taken business courses in high school and typed all her papers even when the teachers didn't require it.

He remembered the first time he'd gone to pick her up for a date, her father had patted him on the back and said, "Hold your shoulders up, boy, you're taking my Dorrie out. Be as tall as you are." He didn't know why he slumped like he did.

His own father had never talked to him except when he was drinking and mad. Drinking loosened his tongue. After knowing what his father was like, why had he ever started drinking? The guys, he reckoned. They teased him a lot about being a teetotaler until one-night Jimmy Brook told him it could help forget his father putting bruises on him. Jimmy said when he got bigger he wouldn't have to take it anymore. After that conservation, he did take some drinks. It didn't taste so bad. His mother didn't like it, though, and Dorrie had refused to marry him for a while. She finally told him she'd just have to break him of the habit. The habit was still there. He just hid it from her and the boys.

He hugged both boys closer to him. Thank God for them. He felt such a huge, empty place inside, like somebody had left the place he lived inside of him and took everything with them. The bed was gone and the chairs, the kitchen table and stove.

He didn't hear a word Rev. Hobbs had said. He didn't have to. It was all good stuff, he knew; it was about his wife. The woman he'd lived with for twenty-three years. The angel called Dorrie had left him forever. Well, not quite. He studied Bryce's eyes. They were Dorrie's, looking back at him. And Dan's clenched, steel jaw line. That was Dorrie's, too.He prayed his own prayer quiet-like to himself with his eyes wide open. Help me to quit, God. I want to do that for all she gave me and the boys.

Chapter 32

MAMA'S MEMORIAL

Mama didn't leave the flowers on the grave long. She decided to take them home. Three days after the funeral she told Papa to drive his truck to the grave site. She was going to bring the flowers home and put them in Dorrie's room. She would make a shrine to her daughter she said.

"Abby, these aren't Dorrie's. She never saw these flowers."

"Of course she sees them. Don't be silly. They're beautiful like she was. I'll also put the cards that people sent on the table and mantle"

"How will that help us move on? How will it help Ollie to see that everyday?"

"This isn't about Ollie; it's about Dorrie."

Papa gave up after that. By the time Mama finished with her plan, the bed also held the dress Dorrie was married in. There were pictures framed of every stage in Dorrie's life, her wedding pictures, her boy's pictures.

She invited Ted and others over to see had done. Behind her back they shook their heads, raised their eyebrows and said what a nice job she'd done because they knew that's what she expected. Among themselves they wondered about her.

Ted and the boys made excuses not to come over for dinner or supper after that. Ollie couldn't believe Mama didn't see how it affected her grandsons to be exposed to this on and on. Papa saw Ted wipe his eyes every time he left the house and get back in his truck to go home.

It was suffocating. That's what Papa and Ollie said to each other. They knew it wouldn't do any good to say it to Mama. She seemed to have retreated to another place.

"It really breaks my heart," Papa said in private to Ollie.

Chapter 33

OLLIE'S DREAMS

Ollie woke up with a start, her pajama shoulders and collar drenched again. Why? Then she remembered. She had dreamed about Dorrie. She sat up, shaking her head to clear her thoughts. Swinging her feet over the side of the bed, she sat up, gripping the sides of the mattress. She frowned, looking into the darkness of the room, but she couldn't understand any better. She worried about why she was having dreams about Dorrie. She woke up in such sweats. Was Dorrie trying to tell her something? In the dream Dorrie wore an everyday pantsuit, like she was still looking after business. It was the pantsuit Ollie last saw her in the day of the fire. It had a mandarin collar and green and black print, and she had on a cardigan she kept at the office. Dorrie was approaching her from the trees in the backyard, her arms outstretched to her. It seemed her dead sister was trying to communicate with her.

They said sometimes spirits did that if they were unsettled or worried about something. Well, for a fact Dorrie didn't die at peace with things.

Ollie covered her mouth and closed her eyes when she remembered that horrible day. She had a hard time breathing. The ready tears washed over her face.

"Oh, God, Dorrie, how could you have died like that? You were so good to everybody. You didn't deserve to go like that!"

Then she gritted her teeth and clenched both fits hard against her body.

"God, how could you let it happen to her?"

She had tried to talk to her mother.

"Ollie, don't you know we must not question God's will? He took her to be with him. You can't question God!"

Yes, she could for the rest of her life! God couldn't have willed for her sister who had been like an angel to everybody to burn in a fire! It didn't make sense that God would take her from the little town that needed her so much. And if He did it would have made more sense if He had come and gotten her in a chariot in full view of everybody like he did Elijah. If there was a heaven, Ollie didn't question that Dorrie was there. If Dorrie wasn't there, nobody would be! Nobody had ever been a better person that Dorrie.

Now, Ollie had a hard time going to church. She hadn't bothered to tell her mother that. It wouldn't do any good. She thought she would be mad at God the rest of her life unless He could somehow explain things to her.

Lately she had heard that sometimes you could talk to the dead person you love in a meeting. She was going to look up the fortune teller's name and call her. That was it. Enough of this sitting around and being mad. That was eating her up on the inside.

She stood up and reached down for her robe on the foot of the bed. Slipping it on she tiptoed out of her room in Mama's house. She didn't want to wake them and have to explain her dreams again. That's why she was in their house now.

When she reached the kitchen, she walked to the back door to look into the backyard at the woods. No Dorrie. Just in her dreams. She bit her lip, wiped her face with the dish towel and watched the hazy sun rise in the east, touching the trees with a rosy glow and breaking the darkness.,

Chapter 34

DONALD AND OLLIE

"Back off, back off, Donald!!"

Ollie swung around to face him and held up both her wet hands like stop signs in front of her. She pointed her forefinger at him while backing herself across the kitchen.

She'd been washing potatoes to peel at the sink when he'd sneaked up behind her and goosed her side.

"Oh Ollie, I was seeing if you were as ticklish as I remember."

"Yeah, Donald, but I'm not five anymore!"

"I know," he said and raised his eyebrows at her while easing his hands in his pants pocket to mollify her.

"I'M YOUR SISTER, DONALD!"

"My half-sister, Ollie."

"Same difference."

She dropped her head and then looked back up. He was still standing there.

"Go ask some girl in town out, Donald. You've divorced, now." She pulled her back up straight.

"Well, who would you suggest?"

"How about the undertaker's daughter, you know, Gloria? Guys are afraid to ask her out. There'd be no competition."

Donald chuckled, "I reckon I see. If he got mad, she could knock him off, and her daddy could bury him fast. No one would ever know…

Something made Ollie shiver.

"I'm going to get a sweater." She turned to go to her room.

"I didn't mean to make you mad." His voice was soft.

She stopped walking but didn't turn.

"Keep your distance." The straight of her back told him he better.

"Thanks for the tip about Gloria." He remembered Gloria now. Good looking woman.

Maybe that wasn't a bad idea.

Chapter 35

GLORIA

Gloria heard the front doorbell to the funeral home ring. She tucked one gleaming black strand back into the French twist, checked her hose seams and walked precisely along the center of the wine-colored with white lilies and green ivy hall runner until she reached the large Victorian side mirror in the hallway. There she turned, smiled at her reflection, turned back, walked ten more steps, kept the smile and opened the huge, curtained, leaded glass door.

The suited man, standing there smiled back at her, revealing a set of long side dimples. His soft brown eyes and black, shining hair captured her attention.

"I'm Gloria McHenry. May I help you? Come in."

"Hello Miss McHenry. I'm Donald Fuller."

She stepped back on stilt heels, pulling the door open to allow him to enter.

In a flash Donald took in her fine figure and inhaled deeply.

"I hope you can help me. But not with a funeral."

"No,?" she questioned.

"My sister actually recommended you," Donald ventured.

"But not to plan a loved one's funeral?" Gloria continued questioning.

She's quick, he thought.

"Well, she said you were excellent at a very hard job. She said she admired you for doing it. She said she wouldn't be able to do it."

"That's interesting." Gloria still sounded puzzled and turned to check a bent flower in a silk arrangement. She straightened it and turned back to him.

Grab her, she's drifting, thought Donald.

"Actually, she said I should ask you out."

Gloria's eyebrows shot up.

"But we don't even know each other. I just met you."

"But we have started the process."

"Maybe," Gloria acknowledged.

"And if you're free at 6 or 7 we could continue the learning process over supper."

Gloria liked the word learning used this way.

"Who's your sister?"

"Ollie, Ollie Sullivan." Donald noticed an immediate softening in her expression.

"Oh, Ollie, yes. She's such a sweet person. A down-to-earth girl. I admire her tenacity for doing things. So you're her brother. Where have you been? Why haven't I seen you before?"

Whoa. So Ollie was an inroad. O.K. He'd never have thought of that.

"I've been living and working away from the community for ten years. You know how you leave the little hometown and you're going to make it in the big city."

"Sometimes," Gloria inserted, "but I stayed here."

"And obviously did very well." Donald smiled.

"My father has made a dependable living."

Donald looked around with appreciation.

"And taught you all he knows, right?"

"Actually, yes, I learned from the ground up… Dad had no sons to tach it to."

"You were smart to let him teach you. Children can learn so much from their parents if they're willing.

"Did your father teach you your life's work?"

"No, he wanted me to stay and learn farming, but I moved away and learned a trade in the city.

"I married a woman who taught he high living, then regretted my decision, and now I'm back without the woman. She wouldn't come back here."

"You mentioned dinner?" Gloria wondered if this man were the prodigal she'd heard about.

"Yes, can I see you about 7 and we get more acquainted?"

"I think so."

Donald extended his hand and noticed how unlike Angela's big hand it was. Small, white, a perfect fit in his.

He also noticed the color high in her cheeks. Good sign.

Chapter 36

GALVESTON SPEAKS
HIS MIND

Galveston stood at the podium and looked at the passage he was to speak on this morning. He cleared his throat and began to read:

"From Ephesians 5:22-24: "Wives submit yourselves to your own husbands, as to the Lord. For the husband is head of the wife, as also Christ is head of the church; and He is the Savior of the body. Therefore, just as the church is subject to Christ, so let the wives be to their own husbands in everything."

"Folks, can you imagine how much trouble a man could get in if he thought this was the end of the discussion? If he quoted or held this over his wife's head to get what he wanted when he wanted?"

"Some religious leaders or preachers have used these verses and others to outlaw women from places of leadership in the church, saying only men should hold those positions. Some men have used these verses to make their women buckle under or obey their whims. As we read in the paper the other day physical abuse was done in the name of the Bible and the church by a man who said his wife did not obey him.

On the other hand, some women have read this passage and become so angry at Paul they wanted nothing else to do with him. So, neither the male or the female types I have just described bothered to read further to verses 25, 28, 29, 33 where it says:

"Husbands, love your wives, just as Christ loved the church and gave Himself for it…"

"so husbands ought to love their wives as their own bodies: he who loves himself."

"For no one ever hated his own flesh, but nourished it and cherishes it, just as the Lord does the church."

"…let each one of you in particular so love his own wife as himself, and let the wife see that she respects her husband."

"So, friends, if we follow the Scriptures in context we will do much better interpretation of them. And that means male and female alike. We will love and respect each other accordingly, like we want to be treated."

Ellie Ann Trotter, a teenager on the second row raised her hand.

"Yes, Ellie Ann."

"Preacher, what do you think personally about women not being able to wear make-up, or combs in their hair, or dresses with pretty colors? God put a lot of color in the world, didn't he?"

"Ellie, that's a very good question, and, yes, He did. Will you give me some time to think about that? Your question deserves some thorough research, maybe a whole sermon, O.K?"

"Yes, preacher. Thank you." Ellie was turning to her mother and smiling.

"And the children so you don't feel left out, the very next verse is Ephesians 6:1. It says "Children, obey your parents in the Lord, for this is right. But that's another sermon for another Sunday."

Galveston was feeling pretty good about the feedback he was getting on the sermon until Bobby Sizemore looked him straight in the eye when he was leaving and asked, "What if a parent is telling you the wrong thing to do and you know it/" He invited the kid to visit him at the church one afternoon after school because that question really bothered him.

Chapter 37

GLORIA'S DILEMMA

Gloria woke up with a start. Why did it seem much later than it probably was.? She flipped over to look at the clock. Nine-thirty! Because it was later. What in the world?

Her father always called her by 8:00 a.m. If he had, she surely hadn't heard or else had gone back to sleep. Oh, dear. Starting out late was not something Papa did well.

Oh, God she was tired. The two of them had stayed up late last night, embalming Mr. Flannagan in preparation for the funeral tomorrow morning. The family was supposed to stop by today to see if everything was alright. The son was bringing a favorite suit for his father.

She tried to flatten her back against the firm mattress to rest it, but it felt like it was permanently bent in the position she'd been in last night to reach the body.

Her eyes scanned the room. When, she thought, would she ever get time to decorate her bedroom like the rest of the building? When, indeed? She was weary of the straight plain nylon panels that matched the plain white walls. The only attempt at color had been the lavender satin ribbons for tiebacks and the lavender pillow shams for her bed. The comforter was even white.

The purple irises with the deep yellow were blooming on the stained glass, hanging in the long, tall bedroom window. Mr. Hutchins at the general store had made that a gift to her for the fine work she did on his wife's funeral. When he'd brought the gift, he'd paused.

"Gloria, you need to look at something cheerful sometimes. You and your Dad see so much sadness. All sadness, girl. I don't know how you do it. Your Dad, now, is all business, but you aren't even twenty-five years old yet."

He stopped talking there but thought further. Not married, hadn't seen the world or much of down the road even...

She sat up on the side of the bed and swayed from side to side trying to get the kinks out of her back.

"O.K. Gloria, rise and shine. If you can't shine, just rise." She rarely shone early in the morning. She picked up her long, white seersucker robe with yellow daisies on it. Onto her long, slender pale arms. Facing herself in the mirror she picked up a red lipstick and ran it over her mouth. Dad had told her one time, and she'd never forgotten it.

"Honey, always put on lipstick when I see you in the morning. I can't bear for you to look pale."

She didn't smell breakfast when she got to the top of the stairs. Maybe he'd had an emergency.

She called out "Papa." No answer. No sound of customers, either.

Well, no mind. She'd go ahead and get her shower and get dressed.

He may have had to go out to get some supplies. That way she'd be ready for the day.

Twenty minutes later she was completely showered and dressed and headed downstairs again when she happened to look up to the end of the second floor. Her father's bedroom door was shut. He always opened it before he went downstairs. He'd overslept, she thought.

She ran in the high heels to the end of the hall, burst in the door without knocking.

"Papa, Papa, you overslept! It's o.k. I'm dressed. I can go down and start. I'll even make breakfast. She kept babbling even as she saw him lying so still, as she bent over him and pressed her fingers to his neck and found no pulse.

"Papa, Papa" as if she could call him back from where he'd gone.

"Daddy, Daddy" as if she called by a different name he'd hear her.

She fell to her knees on the floor and lay her beautifully coiffed head on his chest. Clutching at the covers around his shoulders she sobbed her pain out. Later when Mrs. Flannagan and her grown children found the door to the parlor locked, they drove immediately to Main Street to the Fire Department.

"We found the funeral parlor locked," she started. "Have you heard of his taking a trip? We had an appointment at 10:30. We thought locked doors were unusual."

Chad, the youngest of the firemen, the one who'd found Dorrie in the fire didn't even think twice. He knew it was strange. You could set the clock by Mr. McHenry.

He grabbed his tool belt containing his hatchet off the wall. "Haven't heard of any trip, ma'am. I'm going around there with you."

Chapter 38

LILLIE, THE FORTUNE TELLER

Lillie had never been able to see what her own future would be like. Perhaps that was why she was still single. So also, it might have been why she told fortunes for a living. It gave her a sense of power at least for others to ask her opinion about their lives.

Her mother had controlled most of her waking moments when she was a child. She told her the answers to her questions before Lillie asked them.

So to have her own life she'd moved to Sweetwater. Maybe here there would be an opportunity. Certainly there weren't shingles for fortune-tellers or palm readers or psychics hung out in front yards like in her hometown. She often fantasized about becoming the only fortune teller in Sweetwater.

Her mother had protected her from everything, she thought... mosquitos, poison ivy, measles, bad hair, infections from pierced ears, hay fever, falls from ponies, bad boys by the obvious way, "don't go near, etc." If she got a rash, she put white cotton gloves on Lillie so she wouldn't scratch in her sleep.

So Lillie had moved to a county where there were Olympic-sized mosquitoes, rampant poison ivy, wild ponies, latent immunizations, and dyed hair galore. She only didn't know about the young men yet.

Initially she told every customer to "be careful' as he or she left. When one looked back and said "What?" she stopped. That "be careful" business was a sure carryover from her mother.

She loved her mother but she had to learn to live. She already knew how to be careful. She knew when her mother said "I don't even like to think about that!" what she really meant was she thought about it all the time!

The day that Ted, a widower this year, all sad, came in to ask her what his future was going to be, she described the woman who was going to enlarge his life. She would have long, abundant brown hair, deep blue eyes, a willowy body, and a serious nature. Ted heard her, but she didn't think he realized she was talking about herself.

Today, in fact, the long, lavender-flowered cotton skirt that swirled about her was aggravating the heck out of the poison ivy on her legs.

"Grrrr," she growled as she tried to scratch discreetly.

"What?" said Ted who sat across the silk-draped card table from her.

Chapter 39

THE SÉANCE

She had covered the circular table in the center of the room with a dark green cloth. Now she whisked it off and left the dark mahogany bare. Nothing should interfere with anyone receiving a message from the spirits. She stood one candle in each of the windows of the room. Nearer the time she would light them. Were they to beckon the spirits? She wasn't sure. Boy, if she didn't get some confidence from somewhere she better not do this. Other than a chair for each person around the table, she knew of no other special preparations she had to consider. Were you supposed to serve refreshment at a séance? She didn't know that either. This was her first one. She'd never attended one or read of any. She should have been to one first, before doing this. She knew that now. Things had to be just right.

Well, how many séances would people in this neck of the woods have been to, anyway? Probably none. So maybe she was safe to wing it. Gloria had thought so. No one would mess around with the dead without knowing what she was doing. Gloria was an undertaker. Wait a minute. What was she, Lillie, doing, if she wasn't messing around with the dead? Dead spirits, anyway. Oh, boy, she had to quit thinking like this. She'd never pull it off. She should have made sure to invite Gloria. But, Gloria had told her she'd be fine. Not to worry.

Lillie had met Gloria at church one of the first Sundays after she moved to Sweetwater. One thing led to another and they finally had lunch at the Calla Lily. Oven toaster chicken salad sandwiches and homemade vegetable soup, Gloria had said since they were in related businesses they should look out for each other. No one had ever said anything that important to Lillie before. Of course, she'd never been in any business before. Gloria made a lot of sense. She said it was important in a small town to be in a church every Sunday. That was where you met prospective clients. She had even given Lilly the idea of having a séance. To boost her fortune-telling business, she'd said. To broaden the services, she offered. Lilly felt God had led her to Gloria in this little town where she knew no one. Gloria had even said she'd help her put names with faces. What a friend!

So, where, was all the confidence Gloria had given her?

O.K. She was back on track, now. She paused in front of her oval mirror near the front door. Did she look the part? Who knew? She had chosen the dark purple taffeta skirt and blouse. A scarf surrounded her long, curly brown hair. She'd worn circular earrings dangling for effect. That felt wrong. She stood taller, removed the scarf and the bangle earrings. Too gypsy. Unsophisticated, Gloria would probably say. She strode into the bedroom to the bureau and chose a long necklace of light-colored lavender beads from the top shallow drawer. With practiced fingers she placed the small single matching bead earrings in her pierced ears then looked in the mirror and nodded at herself once. Glancing around she observed the bedroom was straight and left, clicking off the light switch.

In the hallway she parted the bead curtain to enter the parlor and felt they were a nice touch. People would feel these were authentic, passing through them.

It would soon be dark. You had to wait for dark, didn't you? No self-respecting spirit would walk around in broad daylight. Peering through a front window she noticed that the poplar tree in the front yard had lost its last lovely yellow leaves on the ground around it. The camellia bushes boasted some early red flowers, single petal, and her holly tree some red berries. No one would see all these in the dark. Oh well, this wasn't a garden tour. They had not been plantings to boast about, anyway, but former owner's, Mr. Seward. She was usually fond of the black iron gate and fence he had surrounded the yard with, but tonight it gave her a chill. Shivering, she went to the kitchen and boiled water for raspberry tea and toasted a cheese sandwich. Her stomach felt too unsettled for her to eat much, but she felt better when she'd eaten.

Restless, she walked back through the parlor to the front heavy-glassed door. She turned the knob. It was a little loose. She stepped out on the porch as dusk began to fall. There were the usual country night sounds. A lone dog in the distance, howling, probably at the huge pale yellow moon that was rising. There weren't the city sounds of traffic, fire trucks, or police cars. Just the crickets, occasional tree frogs and more wind than usual. One owl answering another owl. A wind blew her hair forward across her face. She pulled it out of her eyes and turned to go back in the house to light the candles. She thought she'd also raise the windows some to let the breeze in. As she went to get the matches from the kitchen, it occurred to her for the first time that neighbors closer than a mile away would have been nice.

Chapter 40

THE SÉANCE BEGINS

Ted, Ollie, and Leona arrived at 7:30 sharp. He had picked the two women up to bring them or else he and Lillie would have had a twosome séance. That would have been fine with him except he realized Lillie was looking to make some money off this séance. Neither Ollie or Leona were big payers of attention to time. Ollie was still resentful at age thirty-five her mother's admonitions to be on time. Leona, since her husband had died, just believed "time passes." She was in no more hurry for anything. After all, she had run behind Harry for fifty years and said she wasn't going to any more fires period. Harry had always had to be early for everything so he could sit there and complain about all those who were late. Ted didn't really blame Leona. He had seen Harry on the scene for two fires before the volunteer firemen got there. When Harry commented how long they were getting there, one of the firemen said well, then, why hadn't Harry already put it out? Ted had thought he was going to have to referee a fight.

Bryce and Dan had begged to drive themselves in Dorrie's car to the séance and Ted had relented. Ted felt guilty now that they were still waiting on the boys. Especially since Dan just had a permit.

"Come the back road to Lillie's now. Don't get caught." He'd told them.

He had finally told Lillie she could start without them.

"I hate to do that, Ted; after all, if you are late to a séance, there's no point going.

I mean, you are paying for this service."

After another fifteen minutes, Lillie had another idea. "I could just charge half for them." Leona was about to drink up all her raspberry tea.

"How much will I owe you, Lillie?"

"Just $15 apiece, Ted."

Stay late, boys, he thought. Whew. He only had $60 total on him. "That's fine.' He'd thought about ten apiece. By George, he wouldn't let a woman's beauty distract him from getting the facts next time. Or maybe he'd propose $10 each since this was her first séance.

Lillie stood up from the love seat. "Let's all take a seat around the table in the center of the room. While ya'll do that, I'll light the candles in the windows."

Ted watched as she moved from window to window. She raised each window as she lit each white storm candle. As the breeze entered the open windows, it blew her hair back from her face. He noticed the way the candlelight added color to her cheeks.

"I'm going to turn out the other lights in the room, now. We'll do the séance with only candlelight."

She moved noiselessly around the room, touching light switches. No one spoke. Finally, she joined them sitting in the second of the three empty chairs. Where was Gloria? She had said she'd come… after Lillie finally called her.

"Everyone put your hands, palms down on the table. That's right."

"All of you have expressed a great desire to be in touch with Dorrie. Maybe she'll be drawn to us with all of our attention on her. Maybe she'll have a message for us. Let's very quietly think of the last time we spoke to her. Focus on that."

The quiet and thick darkness in the room raised the hairs on Lillie's arms. Everyone had shut their eyes without being told to. All you could hear was the clock ticking.

When it seemed to her like it had been long enough, and she should announce that she would give them a rain check for another time, suddenly there was a big gust of wind that came in the back window near the door. What sounded like a voice whispering surrounded the table.

"She's here." Ollie announced it very matter-of-factly.

Ted thought she might be right. The hair on the back of his neck stood up. There seemed like an actual bodily presence back of him and oh, God, hands on his shoulders. He was vaguely aware of car doors closing, footsteps, on the porch, the front door opening.

"Come in, take a seat here at the table. Place your hands palms down and be very quiet. We think she's here." Lillie said to the boys as they entered accompanied by Gloria. "Holy Mother of God, "one of the boys breathed. They moved the chairs out from the table and sat on either side of Lillie.

"That's not appropriate language, boys. You know better," Leona admonished them

"It's o.k." Lillie whispered to Dan.

Gloria took the last empty chair. The wind still swept around the room.

"Jumping Jehosaphat!" Leona spit out. She felt icy fingers touch her wrist.

"Is that a curse word, Aunt Leona?"

"There's a danger...Be tough soldiers"

And then utter quiet. Utter quiet. No one spoke. But Lillie knew somehow now she was gone.

"I'm going to turn the light back on and we'll discuss what's happened."

"Good, good!' Leona offered. "I couldn't understand what she said. You know my hearing problem."

"I heard her," Ollie announced triumphantly. "No mistake. She said, "There's danger.

Be tough soldiers."

"And what does tough soldiers mean?"

"Just that." Ollie turned to Ted. "When Dorrie said that to me when we were growing up, it meant be brave."

"What danger was she talking about?" Ted's face was white and drawn. "Why didn't she explain?"

"Maybe we broke the spell when we interrupted, when we came in late, I'm sorry, I had to call the boys to come and get me. The car wouldn't start." Gloria was being apologetic. That was rare, then Lillie saw how still Gloria was. "But I did hear what she said," her friend added.

"We all did, I think." Leona's eyes frowned, but she was nodding.

They all nodded, but no one got up right away, even when Lillie had cut on all the lights.

Chapter 41

SALE ON SEANCES

Lillie sat thinking about last night's "successful" séance. She enjoyed the warmth of the winter sun through her living room window and looking out at the holly and crepe myrtle berries in the front yard. Not a lot else bloomed or provided color this time of year. The holly berries were bright red, and the crepe myrtle's dark brown, but still berries. The birds were attracted to the red ones but ate both.

Just at that moment a "Caw, caw" called to her from higher up. She craned her neck to see "Heckle and Jeckle" the names she'd given the two crows who frequented her yard. They strutted so arrogantly across the driveway. Lillie had to laugh out loud at them. Even though she tapped on the glass to get their attention, they simply looked up and did not fly away.

"Reckon I attract the dark creatures," she mused, remembering the owl who awoke her often during the night.

Is that how she'd had a successful séance in spite of her lack of expertise? Were unsettled spirits drawn to her? Is that why Gloria wanted her for a friend? What an idea! Was that why she liked Gloria?

These thoughts chilled her, and she turned her back so that the sun's rays penetrated her cloth blouse.

It was lonely here. She had finally resorted to talking to the birds and summoning dead spirits. At least maybe Dorrie was not a dark one, but hopefully one who'd shed light on things that were happening or had happened. She turned again on the window seat. Holding the warm teacup in her hands, looking outside. Against the vivid blue sky, the tall pines stood still. Only small, splotchy white clouds blew along.

"What you need to do is advertise a sale on séances and readings!' Now she was talking to herself out loud. Oh, well, so. She'd post the sign she'd make trimmed in gold and red holly berries and green leaves in the front yard and it would say "Successful séance just last night!' That might help pay the bills she knew the mailman would soon be delivering.

Chapter 42

LILLIE BY HERSELF

Lillie sat in the parlor twirling her hair around her right forefinger and studying the television screen but not seeing what was on. She was already doing what her Aunt Winnie did every night and she was a third of her age. She glanced down at the t.v. tray and wondered why she hadn't just made a sandwich. Half her supper was still there.

She had wanted to be the big, independent do-it-on-your-own person. Well, she had succeeded at the do-it- on her own for sure. There wasn't anybody else under this roof but her, not even a bird or an animal.

She had just studied her books and wondered how long she could keep up this irregular income thing. Sometimes she did very well. The sale on séances sign had brought in some business. The fortune-telling had picked up a little and the tarot cards but nothing regular. Perhaps she'd chosen an undependable trade. Well, so, the construction trade was seasonal and so was school-teaching. She just needed to work on a way to draw business all year. She'd been going to church looking for contacts like Gloria had said.

More than one person had raised her eye brows when she'd explained she was a fortune-teller. She supposed there was still some prejudice attached to her trade. Like she was a gypsy who stole? Looks like they'd seen the substantial little house and known she was no fly-by-nighter. She didn't even own a tent. If she did she'd used it for advertising, not camping.

She'd hoped for Ted to come back by, but he hadn't. Even wished for him to call, ask her out. He probably smiled like that at every pretty girl.

She was still pretty, wasn't she? People used to tell her so. Had he even known she liked him? She thought so. Well, his wife hadn't been dead but six months or so. She reckoned she shouldn't even be thinking about him that way. Was it simply because she was lonely?

She might not have moved out here if she had known it was going to be so deserted most of the time.

Her biggest company by night was still the hoot owl. By daytime she put out bread and seed for the birds, and they didn't disappoint her. All kinds, thrushes, mockingbirds, orioles, redbirds, bluebirds, and Heckle and Jeckle. But she was like the little girl who came by one day with her mother and saw all the birds in her front yard.

"I want to hug a bird, Mommy. I want to hold one."

She'd bought a body pillow, but it didn't breathe so she turned it into a cushion for her bench.

She needed something or someone to hold, to show affection to. She wondered if Gloria was home tonight. She didn't have anybody, either, that she was close to. There was her Dad, but he and she didn't really talk anything but business. Gloria had not welcomed Donald's attention to her so he'd backed off probably thinking she was strange from the profession she was in. Who knew why people didn't persevere in a relationship that given a little time might flourish. She wished she'd had a fighting chance with Ted. She wouldn't back off no, sir.

She moved to the dark brocaded seat beside the black phone and dialed Gloria's number. No answer at Gloria's. She must have gone to the café for supper.

Maybe she should get a dog. That was it. A dog to sit by her chair, watch television with, eat with and sleep on the hooked rug by her bed. That would at least be some company.

"Brrng…ring…ring." She didn't believe the phone was actually ringing.

"Hello, this is Lillie."

"Lillie, this is Mary. I wanted to ask a favor."

"Sure, Mary, what do you need?'

"It's not me, dear, it's Gloria. She needs you, asked for you. Her father died this morning."

Chapter 43

SEARCH LINE

Ollie sat in the front porch swing at Abby and Billy's house. She had been moving back and forth for a while, not thinking much. Just moving her body was some kind of comfort. Looking down at the empty seat beside her she remembered. Dorrie used to sit beside her and they'd swing and solve all the problems. Did moving in a swing loosen your jaw? Maybe if your body was moving you could talk easier. She had done a lot of clamming up recently. There'd been nobody to talk to that she wanted to talk to about her worries. Donald always offered, but she said no thanks.

A full feeling welled up in her throat and heart. She tried to swallow the tears, but it didn't work. There were too many of them. So, she just let them fall. Soon the front of her dress was soaked. She began to feel like a spectacle when she noticed cars beginning to turn down the road in front of the house. It must be store-closing time. She stopped the swing to stand up and go check dinner. A horn being stopped her. When she turned to look she saw Lillie.

"Hey, Ollie, you are the very person I was looking for."

"Me?"

"Yeah, I've had you on my mind."

"Really?" Ollie knew she didn't hear that often.

"You want to sit out there?" Ollie so admired Lillie's little car in her driveway and Lillie having her license.

"Well, what I really had in mind was if you weren't busy, I'd take you to supper with me and we could visit." Lillie's eyebrows went up in a question mark.

"Oh, Lillie, I'd like that. I'll turn the stove eyes off. I've finished their supper, but I have to change my dress. The front of this is soaked. I splashed water on me peeling potatoes. Come inside to wait; it's cooler."

Ollie held the screen for Lillie. "I'll be right back."

"No hurry, there's no man waiting on me. "Lillie stepped inside the front hall and turned right into the parlor. She looked around. She bet nothing had changed in here in fifty years. Her eyes fell on the picture of Dorrie on top of the upright piano. She looked to the other side to find one of Ollie. Not there. But there was a candlestick on either side. Around the room there were pictures of Abby and Billy on their anniversary and the grandkids. Finally, she saw it, a snapshot of Ollie and a man, Lillie figured it was one of her husbands since they were in Sunday dress. There were doilies placed just so on the couch. And no dust.

Then she heard steps on the wood hall floor and Ollie was back. Lillie noticed she had blue combs in her hair and pink lipstick.

"Hey, you look mighty nice."

"Thanks, Lillie."

"Answer me a question, Ollie."

"Sure."

"Do you play the piano?"

"Well, not when anyone can hear me."

"Aha, I thought so.'

"You remember what Dorrie said to me during the séance?"

"That tough soldiers thing?" Lillie puzzled.

"Yes," Color had come to Ollie's face.

"Well, when I came in to dust the piano the other day, a song sort of came to me."

"And you can play it for me now..." Lillie prodded.

"Well."

"There's nobody but me, Ollie. Please."

"O.K. It's sort of. And the woman sat down at the piano and played a definite tune.

"like that."

"Your mothers never heard this, has she Ollie?'

"No."

Why not? Lillie thought.

"You hear her play."

"Well, yeah, but she's practiced and played for years. She's played for church for a long time."

"Ollie, you can play by ear and write tunes. Not everybody can do that. That's a gift. Did your sister play?"

"I don't think so, but she did everything else…"

"I've heard," Lillie mused aloud.

"Ollie you need to play more often that just when you dust! Promise?"

"O.K. I promise."

Lillie watched a huge smile light Ollie's face.

Ollie didn't remember her feet going down the steps. She felt she'd floated to the little car.

When they arrived at The Calla Lily, they saw Gloria eating by herself.

"Hey, Lillie. I called earlier to see if you wanted to eat supper."

"Sure, come over and join us, Gloria. I went to see Ollie to see if she wanted to come to supper. I wanted to offer her a free séance."

Ollie looked up, surprised.

" Really, I second that. You couldn't mistake hearing Dorrie speak to her that night we were at your house."

"You heard it?" Ollie spoke quietly.

"There was no misunderstanding it. Clear as bell." And Gloria patted Ollie's hand and smiled.

"She must really want to communicate with you."

"Gloria… speak softer." Lillie rolled her eyes from the left to right.

When Ollie looked around the restaurant, she worried that the other diners had overheard. No one was talking and some were looking their way.

Chapter 44

ADAM'S DILEMMA

Adam asked his big office a silent question.

If I died tomorrow, what would she do? I can't think about that. That depresses me more than the thought of dying. And she's the one who gets depressed. It's not supposed to be me. The constant buying is what puts us in a bind, but she's just trying to replace the baby with things. I know that. There's no easy solution.

I just have to let her shop when she feels the need. She can't have another baby; the doctor said it was too dangerous.

Worry is making me crazy. He looked down at his hands. I'm biting my nails again. People are going to think I'm a juvenile.

"Ringgg…ring…ring."

"Hello, oh, hello, honey. You had to share some good news? Well, let me have it. I could stand some. O.K. You brought five pair? One in every color? Because they looked so good. I'm glad you found some you liked, Sweetie. I'll see you at six. Right. You don't have to worry about how you look to me. You're always beautiful."

Yesterday it was pillows and toothbrushes in every color. Things could be worse he reminded himself. She could be a kleptomaniac.

"Adam, you look deep in thought. Sorry to interrupt you."

"It's o.k., Fulton. Come on in. It's nothing that has an easy solution anyway."

"Anything you want to talk about?"

"No, I just need to stop worrying about it. I needed an interruption."

"What's worrying you, Adam?"

"How soon we can make a mint. No, just kidding." No, I'm not, he thought.

"Well, I wanted to a question."

"Yes."

"Ollie asked about the water samples again in church yesterday."

"We don't have them yet."

"Well, she's getting anxious like the rest of the congregation."

"What are they worried about?"

"Their drinking water, primarily. Also the wildlife, and the miners, their skin. It seems some of them are having skin rash after being around the dust all day."

"Showers ought to remedy the rash."

"I told them that. But what about the water and the birds and little animals dying around the gypsum mounds."

"Fulton, you know we don't know anything definitive, yet."

"I know. I told them to boil their drinking water to be safe until we get the results back on the water."

"You shouldn't have told them to do that. Fulton. That just makes them more nervous."

"What would you suggest? It's a safeguard and they say they're drinking soft drinks they can't afford to keep buying because they're worried."

"Boiling water has not been recommended by the experts yet. You're telling them that ahead just makes them worry more."

"Adam, I just don't want to be responsible for not advising them if it turns out that there is something to worry about."

"There's nothing to worry about."

"How do you know that?"

"There can't be. That's why. It's simple."

Adam stood up to end the conversation. He knew it wasn't over, however.

"I'll call and check with the county and let you know what they say. Will that make you feel better?"

"It depends on what you find out, Adam. I've lost a lot of sleep thinking about this. Call me as soon as you know."

Chapter 45

SAHARA

Ted couldn't pass by a lady walking on the road. When she realized he had stopped, she looked astonished that he had. Then she took a shy look as she walked over to his truck.

Ted smiled, "Need a lift?"

She nodded.

"Well, get in. Where you headed?"

"You might not want us."

"Us? You and who?" He looked around.

She reached down and picked up a crate.

"Him. A snake."

"Whoa," Ted grinned. "Just sit him in the back."

The young woman walked to the side and hefted the crate into the truck bed.

"Your other bag can go in there on the floor."

"Where you headed?" He asked again.

"Sweetwater. I reckon I'm lucky you're driving a truck."

"Yeah, maybe."

"Everybody doesn't want to carry a snake in his car."

"Yeah, I'll bet."

"Thanks." She smiled again.

"Wow. She was something when she smiled. Even white teeth. A dimple in her chin. Long, swinging brown braids.

"Niles and I, we are expected at the Pentecostal Church this Sunday."

"Church, you're kidding. I thought that he was a pet. You're a snake handler?"

"Right."

"What's your name? I know the snakes."

"Sahara."

"That goes with Nile."

"I thought so."

Ted started to ask then reckoned he didn't want to know how she got this far on foot.

It was like she knew.

"People are kind but then some people in their cars, if they didn't ask, I didn't tell them about Nile. One man heard the snake hiss and thought he had a flat. Then when he didn't he was mad that I hadn't told him. He and his wife told me to get out then."

"I see."

When she started to get out later in Sweetwater, Ted asked, "Where you staying?"

"I believe they mentioned a bed and breakfast."

"Oh, yeah, that would be the Cottonwood Inn. It's three blocks down and turn left, go one block.

Then he felt stupid.

"Get back in. It's no problem to take you there."

"You sure, now?" Her eyebrows went up.

He loved the drawl.

"Sure, it's quick."

"Well, I hope they have a tub. Sahara chuckled. You know I think he's gotten fond of sleeping there. I run some cold-water in. It runs out, but leave some behind for him."

Ted wondered what Ms. Mary McNeill would think of that. And he chuckled.

Chapter 46

SAHARA AND MS. MARY

Sahara walked up on the front porch of the Cottonwood Inn. She carried Niles in his crate, which was a fine woven one, impossible to see in. She had made sure of that. There were some places where she'd certainly not get admission if the innkeeper saw the nature of her baggage. However, if Niles decided to make his presence known, the crate was no insurer of anonymity. He could definitely be heard when he liked to be and there were times he really liked to be seen and heard. Like when he thought Sahara had made him wait too long for a meal. She could be on a diet when she wanted. He, however, had not signed on for a diet, ever. So she tried to feed him on a fairly regular schedule. He required one meat a week, thank you. After all, he was her livelihood. She smiled to herself when she thought of how he liked to remind her of that. No shy, retiring snake, hers.

She tapped on the lace-curtained front door several times. It opened. An ample lady, huffing and puffing, smiled broadly and invited her in.

"Come on in; you didn't have to knock. Everybody's welcome!" She stood back to let Sahara in.

"The name's Mary McNeill; the place is the Cottonwood Inn! Although I'm thinking of a name change."

"You or the inn?"

"That's pretty sharp of you, girl. The Inn's, actually. My husband's the one who named it, and he's no longer here. Took off with the money in the till and a younger woman. That's why I want to rename it."

"Speaking of names, what's yours? And let me get you a cup of tea or a Pepsi."

"Sahara's mine. A Pepsi sounds great; I'm really thirsty."

"Here, let me help you with your bags." Mary reached forward to take the crate. Sahara swung it quickly out of Mary's reach.

"I can manage. They aren't heavy."

"I like your name. I wish my mother had named me something dramatic. Every other girl's name is Mary. It's so ordinary."

Sahara followed her down the hall into the kitchen on the right.

"But it does go well with your last name… McNeill."

"Right you are, and nice of your say so." Mary gestured to chairs at the long oblong table covered with oilcloth. The pattern was of cypress trees and grey moss, but the flower centerpiece was red cockscomb. The back windows looked out of spreading live oaks.

"What brings you this way, Sahara? Mary handed her an ice-cold drink from the refrigerator and a bottle-opener. She pulled the red and black house dress away from her body before she sat down.

Sahara sat Niles over against the wall behind Mary and prayed he was taking a nap. So far so good. She hadn't planned on this interlude.

"Well, the Holiness Church invited me."

"Oh, are you a minister?" Sahara observed Mary taking in her form-fitting sundress.

"No Ma'am, just speaker."

"Well, great, then, I'll have to come and hear it. What's your topic?"

Merciful God. She was going to be kicked out before she got in.

"Animals in the Bible."

"Really, that sounds interesting. Are you an animal expert?"

"More like an animal lover."

At the moment there was a swish, swish in the crate.

Sahara tried mind control. No, Niles.

"What was that?" Mary started to turn in her chair.

"A mouse, I think, I saw something dark streak down the wall."

"Oh, me," Mary rolled her eyes. I do have one occasionally. My cat died."

"Sorry to hear it…" Sahara was actually glad. Mice were Niles' favorite.

"Don't worry, I'm not afraid of them. They make me feel at home."

"Well, let me tell you about meals before I show you your room. I make an eggs and ham breakfast if I know the night before. Sandwiches for lunch if you are here. And meat and two vegetables at supper. I give you a copy of the menu the night before to look at and decide."

"Sounds great." Sahara licked her lips.

"Mary, could I have permission to set a mousetrap in your room?"

"Sure, let me get you one."

"I have my own."

"Really?" This was a first.

"Let me introduce you, Mary." There was no way around it. She would not lie to this lady.

Mary looked out at her quizzically.

"I have my own personal mousetrap in this basket. He is Niles, a handsome rattlesnake.

He will help me with my speech to the church. I will handle him to prove my faith in God."

Mary's eyes had grown enormous. She held her hands up from the table as a guard with palms toward Sahara as if to ward off the reptile that was still secure in the basket.

"Oh, God, Sahara, you're kidding! I've never been used to snakes, …what the heck, I'm scared to death of them! So I can't have him lose. I'm afraid to even look at them. Oh, and I was liking you so much, hoping you'd stay a while. Ohh…"

Sahara felt remorse as she looked at the woman's fear, heard the nervous chatter that proved it. She hadn't felt sorry about duping anyone before.

"Mary, I'm so sorry I didn't tell you first. I was just afraid you wouldn't let me stay if you knew about Niles. I like you, too. We hit it off. Please, is there any way I can stay if I keep him fastened in his basket? He has had his poison removed. That's the most important thing, isn't it? Of course, that's a secret between us. If I don't let him out around you, and he's no longer poisonous, can I stay?"

"I suppose you do have a hard time finding somewhere to stay…"

"Yes, I do. Getting a ride, too."

"Is this your only job, Sahara? Whew! How did you get into this line of work?"

"An uncle of mine showed me how to handle snakes. Later, when I couldn't stand staying at home anymore because mom and dad were always gettin' into violent arguments, he let me take one on the road with me, said I could probably make a little at churches this way."

"Amazing!" Mary thought back to her simple, rather boring childhood, so predictable from week to week. Her mother and father lived in town, her mother running a boarding house, her father working at photography in one of the front parlors of the house. They had not known what was wrong with him when Mary was small. Some days he couldn't work; he was so depressed, he hardly got out of bed. Other days he was unstoppable, making his appointments until all hours. His work on some of those days had made some national publications. It was outstanding. The color and light, the expressions on his subjects.

Mary had been envious of her father's talent. Her mother's work was so mundane. But she had inherited her mother's gift of gab and she easily learned her cooking skills.

"Mary, I promise I won't let Niles out in the bathtub like he likes unless I am in the room with him with the door locked. How's that?"

"Sahara, let's take it on a 'we'll see basis." Mary wondered if this situation might just help her with her spells of depression she'd inherited from her dad. Thankfully, he'd also had a sense of humor which blended with her mother's tolerant gene. Yeah, she surely was a mix of them both.

"Wonderful, Mary, you surely are a reasonable person."

"Well, I have to be honest Sahara; life's been pretty lonesome for me lately. Any change at all would be better."

"I hope so, Mary. You might even learn to like Nile."

Mary's eyes rolled again skeptically, but she didn't lose the smile.

Chapter 47

SOUND EFFECTS

The storm that day started easy... thunder, lightning, a few miles off. Herb was only vaguely aware of it. He was busy preparing collards to cook; he always washed them three times to get all the grit and sand off.

Jacqueline hadn't come in today. That left him to do it all. She was so undependable. Working hard one day she'd impressed him. The next day she would not show up. Sometimes, she'd call late to tell him she was sick. He had no one to replace her. He'd spoken to her, but unreliability was her trademark. He'd finally reorganized the pattern. She must think those fishnet hose and wispy hairdos made up for it. That might work on some men, not on him. A loud crack outside made him finally look up from the sink and notice the lightning. Probably because the lights flickered.

"Oh, no," he said aloud to himself, "not while I'm getting supper ready. Thank goodness, I made chicken salad early."

In moments there was a virtual deluge outside, the rain coming down so hard you couldn't see across the street. He turned off the water and reached for the colander hanging above the island. When he was grabbing the last double-handful of collards, he heard the front door open, ringing the bell.

Jacqueline, is that you?" He called out.

"It's just me, Herb, Ollie. Can I come in from the rain? I feel like a drowned rat. It came up so sudden. Boom! He looked up to see her sprawled on the floor.

"Oh, goodness, Ollie, are you alright? He ran around the counter and reached his arms down to help her up.

"Here, this water is what made you slip! Let me go get some towels. Sit down right here."

He pulled a seat away from the nearby table.

He dried his hands on his apron. He turned around to go to the storeroom closet in the back of the café and brought back several hand towels for her.

"Whoa, you are wet. Here, take these and dry off. I'm sorry they're not big ones, Ollie. How about I get us a cup of hot tea?"

"Thank you, Herb, I'm so embarrassed." She wasn't lying. Her face was red.

When he got back with the tea, Ollie was drying her hair with one towel. She looked stricken. Like she'd done something wrong.

"Gee, I'm sorry. Nothing like falling in my own puddle, is it?"

"Thank you, Herb."

"Sure, are you O.K? You didn't break anything, did you?"

"No, I am just clumsy, like mama says, I reckon. Frankly I'm glad for the company and the break. Jacqueline didn't show up, so I've had double duty."

Ollie looked around, "Would you like me to help you? I know my way around a kitchen."

"I couldn't ask you to do that, Ollie. You've got stuff to do."

"You didn't ask. I offered. Actually, I'm through with errands. Mama's cooking supper tonight."

"That's really nice of you, Ollie. Very nice. But those wet clothes?" He wanted to say he'd get her something dry to put on of Carlie's from the back, but he couldn't quite get it out. That was complicated.

"They'll dry, Herb, it's hot weather. What can I do first? Put these collards on or start with something else?"

"Be sure your shoes are dry on the bottoms." He turned to get some paper towels, but Ollie was already in the kitchen, studying the collards and looking up at the pots.

"This big one, right?" She asked as she took it down off the hanging rack.

Herb was flabbergasted. No woman but Carlie had ever looked for work to help him with.

"Yes, there's streaked meat for the collards in the refrigerator, Ollie. You can start with those. Thank you. Hey, I'm glad you dropped by."

"I sure did that… dropped in!" She looked at him and they both laughed.

"You sound like you trust me in the kitchen to know how to do it, Herb." Her voice sounded happy and a little puzzled like she wasn't used to that.

"Sure, I do. I heard Donald bragging about Abby's cooking the other day. Didn't she teach you how to cook?"

"Yeah, she taught me a lot. And I taught myself some."

"Good, I get to sample some, then. Lucky for me the rain blew you in today! You're a godsend."

As he said that, Herb glanced in her direction. She was slicing the streaked meat in thick slices and laying it in a frying pan on an eye beside the pot of simmering collards.

"Do you have any white cornmeal, Herb? I could fry some cornbread."

"Wow, sure, comin' right up, Ollie." Herb pulled the bag out of the pantry and handed it to her.

"Hey, this is flour, not cornmeal. Do you have cornmeal?"

It was Herb's turn to be embarrassed. "Sure I do. Why did you do that?"

"Maybe to see if I'm on the ball?" Ollie smiled and exchanged bags with him.

He noticed her eyes were deep blue like the Prussian blue crayon in the Crayola box when he was a kid. Why was he thinking about that?

"Do you want me to cook any of these crowder peas to go with the greens? She was looking in the freezer now.

111

"Perfect, Ollie." What had he stumbled into?

"Hey, how about a snack, Ollie, I'm hungry! I could half one of these apple danishes with you?"

He cut it in two before she answered.

"Yum, I like those." She licked her fingers. "Do you have any dessert made for supper?"

"I haven't yet. There was so much cleaning to do."

"I know a good, quick cobbler I could make with some canned plums if you have any, but you're the cook."

"Plum cobbler would be great. My lemons weren't juicy enough for a pie."

"You just sit out your self-rising and the sugar. I'll get the margarine and milk."

As he turned back from the pantry with both hands full of flour and sugar, she was looking straight at him, like staring, and it startled him. He dropped the sugar and mumbled he was the clumsy one, as he leaned down.

She hurried around to help him get it up, but when she bent down she bumped heads with him.

"Ow..! They both said at once as they rose up slowly.

"What is the matter with us? Ollie? We are a wreck around here, aren't we?" Herb laughed out loud. So Ollie followed suit.

"How long can you stay? I'll pay you!" He said.

"To help you serve and close, how's that, no pay, just supper here?" And there was that little smile again. It went crooked and kind of prim on one side, down. The other side ended up in a big dimple.

"I'd be happy for the company, Ollie, but I'll owe you more meals, if you won't accept pay. Will that work?" He raised his eyebrows.

"You bet," Ollie said, smiled at him, and started humming as she worked.

For the first time in a long time Herb wanted the day to last longer.

Chapter 48

THE WHOLE TRUTH

The hose made Sahara's legs itch. She was more used to socks and tennis shoes or boots. Was she still allergic to nylon? She remembered when she used to have to wear corduroy instead of wool skirts. Wool still broke her out in hives.

As she sat on the front row of the church waiting for her introduction she believed all eyes must be on her or the basket where Niles occasionally swished-swished. For a fact both the young lady in the dark blue and white dress beside her and her little red-headed boy had their eyes on the basket from which quiet sounds were heard.

According to the program Niles and her act, followed the first anthem by the choir, "Cast Your Burden Upon the Lord."

Sweat was running from her armpits to her waist. Had she remembered deodorant? She leaned her head to her shoulder to see if she could catch a whiff. O.K. she smelled the lilac scent.

Why was she so nervous today? Everything was going to go as usual. She surely hoped so. She would say a few words about proving her faith by handling the wild, poisonous, snake in front of them. She'd do just that, then loop Niles back into the basket, even when he tried to get away and refuse to go back in. He liked being out lately.

The next time she did this routine, she was not going to meet and get to be friends with people first. She could do this act better in front of strangers.

Boy, she wished she'd eaten the ham biscuit Mary had offered her this morning. Her stomach was about to growl, thinking about how good it had smelled.

Thank goodness, she'd trapped a mouse last night for Niles. He should be on his best behavior.

Or should he be on his worst? That would probably be better...

"Cast thy burden upon the Lord and He will sustain thee."

He never will suffer the righteous to fall. He is at thy right hand.

Thy mercy, Lord, is great and far above the heavens.

Let none be made ashamed that put their trust in Thee."

The choir in short white robes were sitting down. Galveston stood up, nodding a thank-you to them and walked to the big mahogany lectern.

"There is a major sermon in those four short lines, friends. Did you hear it?"

"Friends, you are in for some excitement this morning. We have a young woman who is anxious to show us the power of faith over fear. The proof of what the Bible says in Mark16: 17-18."

"As you recall, it says in those verses that those who believed would be able to handle serpents without being harmed. May I introduce Miss Sahara Overton from all parts, actually.

She's a travelling handler of snakes."

"Come up to the pulpit, Miss Overton... so we can all see you perform this brave deed."

Sahara reached down to pick up the basket. A loud hiss ensued from it that was probably a communication from Niles. Of what she wasn't sure. But as she walked up the steps and took her place behind the podium, he grew quiet again.

She took hold of the lectern atop the podium and looked down at the expectant face.

Mary's faces beamed a supportive smile, a little to her eyebrows. She liked Mary so much.

She was like the mother she wished she'd had… Warm… How had she thought she could stay on here, though? Her job was to travel, to handle the snake.

Preacher Hobbs was clearing his throat. She had allowed herself to drift off, standing there. What must they be thinking? Actually what they thought was important. More and more.

"Excuse me, folks. I didn't mean to act tongue-tied. I was just thinking how kind many of you have been to me since I've been in town. Mary McNeil provided me a place to live when maybe nobody else would have.

"How many of you, if a girl arrived at your door with a snake in a basket, would you welcome her?"

"The people looked at each other and rolled their eyes and exchanged knowing looks." "And Herb at the café said, "Sure, come right on it. It doesn't have to be a seeing eye dog.

Just keep the lock on the basket hooked!"

There were some chuckles and an "I'll bet."

"And Mr. Gibson at the general store wouldn't sell me a lock for the snake's basket. He said it would be a pleasure to give me one, like a welcome wagon present. Of course, he knew he was doing all of you a favor."

This time there were some hearty laughs. Galveston himself, smiled at the girl's gift of gab. The choir director continued to eye the basket nervously, however.

Sahara herself didn't know exactly where the words were coming from. This wasn't what she'd planned to say.

"Mr. Harris and his son at the drugstore said they trusted me to come in and look around. He said business wasn't so hot anyway, that I might pick it up. Smiles galore.

"And I met Mr. Reynolds at the newspaper. He was chewing the end of his pencil when I walked in. He wanted to do a feature on me and Niles sometime about where we've and what we've done. He said it might up his subscription number."

"And Rev. Hobbs... She turned to look at him...was so kind. He said he'd like Niles and me here every Sunday. That then folks wouldn't go to sleep?"

Again, many laughs. Galveston nodded his head and grinned broadly.

"You've all welcomed me. It's been unbelievable."

Now tears were running down her face. She let them, still holding tight to the lectern. Things became immediately quieter. One could have heard his or her neighbor's heartbeat.

"So I'm going to do something I've never done before, tell you the truth about my snake and me."

"You see, Niles here, she looked down at the basket, has had the poison taken from him."

"He can't hurt you or me."

There was audible whispering.

"He is my pet snake like some of you all have cats and dogs. Five years ago, I had to leave home. It was becoming dangerous to live there because my parents drank and fought.

When I told my Uncle Ray I had to leave and make life my own way, he gave me the idea of snake-handling. He said it was catching on like' speaking in tongues' or people 'getting healed by laying on of hands."

"He told me to give myself a new name, Sahara, because I came from the desert (as far as home life went) and to call the snake he gave me Niles after one of the longest rivers in the world. He had two other snakes. They were both a hobby of his."

"When he saw I was afraid, he told me Niles couldn't hurt me because he had no poison in him anymore but that he'd be good protection for me since I was starting out on my own as a woman. He also taught Niles to give me a hug around the shoulders. That was the clincher. I'd never gotten many of those."

"So now I suppose I've just ruined the show. You won't have to pay me. But I hope I've got a job with Ms. Mary. She's got a new plan to have some rooms of the Inn as room and board."

Niles and I may have found a home after all if Mary will have me. She's gotten over her fear of him. She can even hold him. Would you like to meet Niles?"

Much clapping and a few whistles.

When they subsided, Sahara bent down to open the basket. She turned the combination and removed the lock. When she opened the two doors that had been closed, a handsome long green and brown reptile rose straight up and out of the basket. Slithered up her arm to her shoulders and neck and rested there, curling and uncurling his body.

Many women gasped. The several men on the front row sat straighter. One of them said, "Whoa!"

"Don't be afraid; he's just a show-off. Mary, come show them what you'vel earned. Mary chortled and climbed the pulpit steps, reached and took Niles from Sahara. She looked the snake in the eyes and said, "Sahara has taught me not to be afraid anymore of a lot of things, not just snakes. A year ago I wouldn't have come in this room if I knew there was any kind of snake here. So in a way this demonstration is about conquering your fears by believing in yourself and others. And God? We should believe in him first to help us have courage."

Galveston shook his head in disbelief. He moved to Sahara's left side.

"Folks, the snake's got my tongue. This talk is a sermon in itself. I'll preach today's sermon next Sunday, o. k.? In the meanwhile, if any of you haven't met Sahara, do so soon. Thank you, Sahara and Mary."

Chapter 49

THE CANNA LILV CAFÉ

Herb had not turned around to look at the first time Carly had passed him on the street. It was when he was in her father's restaurant for breakfast, and he heard her talk to a crying child, that he had looked for her to find her. As she said what she did to comfort the little boy who had been spanked for spilling his dinner, he stopped what he was doing to find the special voice. Secretly he cheered as she suggested to the father who towered over her that he shouldn't spank his son for something adults did, too... that a kid would grow up thinking you couldn't make mistakes and would be afraid to try anything.

When he left the restaurant, he said "Way to go, I'm Herb."

She had smiled back and said

"Thank you, I'm Carly."

On his was home he'd thought what a good mother she'd probably make. Later he'd learned she was not married and didn't have children, and he'd gone back again to eat.

One day he'd witnessed two men she was serving taunting her, pulling her hair and patting her backside. He walked over to the table with new-found bravado.

"Excuse me, I don't know where ya'll are from, but you fellows need to apologize to this young lady and act like gentlemen or leave." Her eyes had flashed gratitude and something else. It was Carly and Herb always after that.

He had tried to learn her dreams. She didn't talk about those. She claimed she lived day to day, but he never stopped asking. One day she told him she wished she could write about being a small person... that you didn't have to let it get you down.

She said women had told her she didn't have a figure so what gender was she? And some men had felt they could take advantage like she was a child forever. He had stayed behind her until she wrote her feelings down.

All children, but especially any with a handicap like Jimmy, flocked to Carly. He had had polio, and kids teased him about how he walked. Older ladies liked the respect and attention she paid them. She had told them they were wise and could teach her a lot if she listened.

Chapter 50

CARLY'S CANNAS

Herb took the white ribbed crochetted dishcloth and wiped the counter one more time, letting his thought take over. His wife had made him twelve dishcloths just before she'd gotten sick with cancer. Her voice still echoed in his mind.

"All white, Herb, to look clean, spotless for the diner. Clorox will fix any stains. People wouldn't know if those gray ones are ever clean. They'd see all these are homemade and be impressed." She'd arranged them to look like a lily bouquet and tied green ribbon around them. "You can always say I gave you flowers, can't you?" She'd put her arms around him and kissed him on each corner of his mouth to make him smile. There'd never be another Carly.

The name for the restaurant had come from a picture of red cannas on the front of one of Carlie's flower catalogs.

"Flowers have a happy place in people's lives for the most part, Herb. These are red and grow in this area. Don't you think red's an inviting color? They say it makes people hungry."

She'd been right like she always was. Carly was smart, intuitive, some people said.

She'd been a small woman with smiling brown eyes that had melted his rigid heart.

She always wore her hair in a long, thick pony tail that curved down her back, more hair than a little person like her needed. She had a girl's body but was more giving than most women had more to give physically.

Daredevil, Carly's black satin cat would migrate to his wife's bed pillow every morning and circle his wife's head with his tail like a halo. Herb would wake up to see it, smile, and reach over to tantalize the cat who never failed to lift a paw and make a claw to smack him. Herb would point a finger at him and say, "I dare you." The cat would withdraw, and they'd make necessary peace because Carly loved them both.

Herb felt pain in his chest still from the loss of her. She'd filled his life in so many ways…the warmth of her body backed up to him at night when they slept, the way she always filled his cup or glass, or plate with more than he needed to eat or drink. She knew he'd grown up hard as a migrant farmer's son and skipped a lot of meals. She'd told him she never wanted him to be hungry again. She'd taught him all the recipes her father had used in his restaurant and helped give Herb his start that way. More than that she'd worked by his side from day one and people loved her open heart just as he did.

He had to get out of here. Everyone was gone since supper.

Chapter 51

PAPER HANDS

One day when he came in to see her on his lunch break from the restaurant she was restless and lonely she said, on a break from the usual pain. He sat down on the bed beside her and leaned to kiss both sides of the mouth to make her smile. She had taught him that. Finally she did relax enough to smile.

"Do you want me to go get you a book or a magazine, Carly?" I wish I could just stay here with you. Look, I brought you some rice pudding. It has raisins and cinnamon like you like."

"No, just you, this hour. You're so good for me. You're the first man who ever made me feel special, like I had amounted to something."

"You're good for everybody, Carly; so many people want to know where I found you. I tell them I was really lucky. You were right under my nose. I was just blind at first."

"Do you believe that old saying that there is only one person in the world that you can fall in love with? If so, I found her. I'm a lucky so and so."

"I don't know about that. But you made me feel complete, like someone who could think my thoughts or understand feelings. That I wouldn't have to explain myself with all the time. '

"I know. I can start a sentence and you can finish it." Here Herb had to get up and pretend to be fixing the covers. He would cry if he didn't.

"I'm going to get you some fresh ice water. Be right back." He grabbed the pitcher and glass and hurried to the kitchen.

"Can you bring a couple of those pieces of paper in the drawer by the Silverware? And the scissors. And a pen.?" She called down the hall.

"Sure, anything for my bride." God, why did I say that? He held on to the kitchen table and wiped away tears from his eyes with his shirt sleeve. Taking several deep breaths, he turned to open the drawer she had mentioned. He lay the paper, scissors, and pen on the counter by the sink and turned the water on hard to cover his sobs. In a moment when his throat didn't hurt quite so much, he cut the water off and grabbed the dish towel to wipe his eyes again.

When he took the supplies back in to her, she reached for them and her writing board he'd made her that she kept by the bed.

"You want to sit up for a while? Let me plump up your pillows."

"I had an idea. Put your hands on the paper. Right here." In a moment she was tracing around them.

"What are you doing?"

"You'll see, later. Here's the dish. See, I ate all the pudding It was wonderful.'

He took the dish and spoon, kissed her on the forehead and left without talking. He couldn't. He had just squeezed her knee. She understood.

When he returned later after cleaning up the diner, he found her asleep. She was holding the paper hands of his she'd cut out against her heart.

After many uses, the hands wore out from her kisses. Then she said she had a better idea. She wanted his garden gloves. The day she died he buried those gloves with her, after he intertwined the fingers with hers.

Chapter 52

OPPORTUNITY KNOCKS

The car windshield had two looks. One was sprinkled with raindrops; another was glassy and clear. Where the wipers had swished, it was slick and clean. Either way was alright with Lillie. She sat still, watching the rain fall on the hood of the car and the pavement of the street. Someone tapped on her window.

"You o.k., Lillie?" It was Chad's face at the window. She didn't know how long she'd been sitting there. She knew she'd sat before she went into the drugstore. She liked people-watching, but it did make her sad sometimes when she watched the mothers and children under their umbrellas hurrying and laughing when they splashed one another in the puddles.

The door opened. "I saw your car idling and I wondered if it was giving you any trouble."

What he'd been thinking was that too much of that exhaust might be filtering inside her car.

"Thanks, Chad, it's o.k. "He was the fireman who'd tried to get Dorrie and Cliff out of the burning oil company. "I was just watching the kids play." Why was she lying?

I'm just in no hurry to go anywhere or do anything, she thought.

"Could you give me a ride?" That'll do it, thought Chad. "It started pouring after I got here."

He wondered if she knew she'd been sitting there close to fifteen minutes.

"Sure, be glad to. Where you headed?"

"Back to the firehouse, I reckon. I had to come refill the emergency medical kit we carry on the truck."

"Oh, I see."

Her eyes looked glazed.

"How 'bout I get you a cup of coffee at the diner, Lillie? Are you in a hurry anywhere?"

"Actually, no." She'd forgotten exactly what she'd come to town for.

"Well, good. Stop down at the Cally Lilly. I haven't had lunch, have you? I'd like to get a sandwich."

"Sounds good, Chad. I'm hungry, too." She felt her mouth smile awkwardly.

Chad liked the tenderness that showed around her eyes and mouth when she smiled. Why had he never asked her out? Well, at least he'd been ready for the moment.

A few minutes later they both shook rain from their coats and hair and shoes, and then sat down in the booth Herb showed them to.

Even with damp hair uncombed and wet clothes, a bit bedraggled, she was an attractive woman. She seemed to shed light when you looked a her.

"Rain is definite blessing," he said.

Lillie didn't feel she could ask what he meant.

"Ask me why."

"It waters everything."

"No, well, yes, but that's an obvious answer. Actually it made me ask how you were and then ask you to go to lunch and ask myself why I haven't done this before."

"She started to say he must say that to all the girls but then thought he probably didn't.

"Thank you, Chad."

"Thank you, Lillie."

125

"Am I older than you?"

"Does it matter?"

"Well, no, not really, I suppose."

"You suppose right."

"I'm 30."

"O.K. I'm 27, older that I look, some people say."

"You will probably look young forever, Chad. You have one of those faces."Lillie blushed when she said it and looked down.

Chad couldn't remember when he'd seen a girl blush.

"So we agree that age doesn't matter. What matters is what we think matters."

Lillie jumped in. "Well, I think people matter."

"Me, too, in a big way. So see we agree on something important."

"How have you been?" He saw some sadness lurking behind the smile.

"Pretty good." She wondered if she risked saying she was lonely. Probably not.

"Pretty, yes. I see that. Good. I don't know."

She laughed out loud and he felt good he'd made her laugh.

"Don't mind me. They say I'm a smart aleck. My Mom and Dad, both.

"A nice one, I think."

"I try."

She had heard he was kind-hearted.

"Do you like animals?" She felt a little braver.

"Absolutely. Two things we agree on if you do."

"Do you have a hobby, Lillie?"

"I believe my business is one, since I'm not making much money at it." Why had she said that?

But he was laughing. "I like your sense of humor."

"Do you have a hobby, Chad?"

"Skeet-shooting sometimes, but they laugh at me because I won't shoot the real thing. I reckon metal-working is my real hobby."

"What kind of metal-working do you do?"

Well now, I'll have you over to the house tomorrow to see. Are you up for that?"

His eyebrows rose quite attractively, Lillie thought, and then she said "Definitely."

More quickly than she should have, she was afraid.

Chapter 53

CHAD'S HOBBY

"What is metal-working, Chad? I'm not familiar with that."

"It's different things to different people.'

"What do you mean?"

"Well, one person might like punching tin."

"I've seen that. If you put a candle under a tin cover, the light comes out in spots, but it's very pretty that way.'

"That's good, Lillie. Spots of light."

"Some people like to work with iron that's been heated to a high temperature like in blacksmithing. They mold it into something they want an image of."

"Oh. Is that what you do?"

"No, I like working with smaller pieces, like abandoned tableware. I like making art out of something other people think is not longer useful. It's like recycled into something else."

"Why did you say abandoned?"

"Because it was a big part of their life once."

His folks just shook their heads when he brought home the old silverware from the thrift stores, but they had allowed him to use the garage and turn it into his workshop. Finally he had wired and plumbed it and made it into a studio apartment.

Today, a Saturday, he had invited Lillie over to see his hobby. As he ushered her into the garage, her eyes canvassed the big room and saw all the jars of silver.

"Wow! Hey, I'm short on spoons. You have any extra here?" Lillie's laughter filled the place like notes in a song. Chad noticed her eyebrows were up and her hand went over her mouth in amazement.

He laughed a deep-throated laugh. "Sure, how many do you need?" He wanted to hug her to him. What was that about? He stopped himself from reaching for her.

"How about four?" She giggled again comfortably.

"You've got them. Pick out which ones you want."

He smiled when he saw she didn't pick all the same kind, but four different ones.

"You want to see what I do with this ugly, discarded fork?"

"Oh yes, that one?" She pointed to the one on the work table lying by itself.

"Yes, I picked a plain one on purpose."

He sat down and started by bending the fork with pliers. Picked up others. Bent and connected them. In a half hour he had made what looked like a baby's playpen.

"Chad, that is lovely. Is it what I think?"

"What do you think it is?"

"A baby's playpen? It's so sweet! May I touch it?"

"Sure." He held it out.

She cupped it gently, turning it in her hands, then wondered.

"Can you make a baby?"

"I'm not sure." He raised his eyebrows at her, but she was still looking at the work of art. He remembered that he'd made a silver baby before, from a silver baby spoon.

Chapter 54

ANTIQUE ATTIC

Gloria woke up with a fine idea. She had actually dreamed about it. That meant it was a good one, maybe. At least it was on her mind. They, she and Lillie, if Lillie was interested, would set up an Antique Attic. That was where you found antiques sometimes, wasn't it? She'd sell out all the things that had made this house a funeral parlor and use the money to add more furniture or "treasures", keepsakes, they'd find in a flea market. They could live upstairs unless Lillie wanted to keep her house.

Just the other day she'd picked up a house magazine and seen an idea she loved. An artist had taken old photographs of people she'd found discarded in flea markets and made collages including some of her drawings to express some kind of dream, or goal she imagined that the person had. The collages made her think of all the pictures that were missing from her life. She barely had any of her father and mother, at least not any she'd been able to find. Lillie had offered to help her clean out the third-floor attic. Her father had never wanted to tackle that after her mother died.

God, it was kind of Lillie to say she'd help her… with going through her dad's clothes, too. But that was the way Lillie was. The best kind of friend.

She'd heard Lillie express dismay over how her business was going.

She didn't think Lillie's whole heart was in it. Not the fortune-telling business. No wonder about that. Lillie was too honest a person. Lillie would not have understood her father's financial philosophy.

"It's a means to an end, Gloria, a means to an end," when she objected to some of his charges he made on his bills to people for services. Then he would laugh at the double meaning his own joke had.

Get rid of. Who would want it? Dear God, who would want all the things that make up a funeral business? It wasn't like a restaurant or a hotel going out of business. A person could use beds, drapes, table, lamps sheets, towels, or pots and pans for other personal home use. But the chemical compounds, the huge basins, the stainless tables, the coffins – no way the general public would buy those at a yard sale.

The obvious people might be interested. The other funeral homes in the state. For a moment she felt guilty. People would be expecting her to go ahead with running this business. After all she had spent many years of her life doing that... helping her father run the business. Would she miss it? No, emphatically. She pushed her tongue behind her front teeth to try to stop the tears she felt starting behind her eyes and nose. It didn't work. That was true a lot lately. The doctor said it might be because she'd held a lot of emotions in for so long. She would miss her father. He had been all she'd had. Until Lillie.

The more she thought about it, the more excited she became. She sort of wished Lillie might want to keep her house. She wanted to get out of this one. At least for living in. She would talk to Lillie tomorrow.

She'd call Rowland Funeral Home first. They were in the adjoining county. They'd been very kind on several occasions to her father when he couldn't do a funeral for a local person. They were also a smaller home and probably needed some equipment. She would make them a real deal.

Chapter 55

LILLIE AND GLORIA

Lillie tried to watch Gloria out of the corner of her eye or when she thought Gloria was otherwise engaged and wouldn't notice. Never before had she met a woman she admired as much or wanted so much to be like. She was not like some woman wanting to catch the other woman in a mistake so that she herself would be superior somehow. She was just basically in awe of Gloria. She wished she had Gloria's savoir-faire if that was the word. Gloria knew how to dress, how to talk, how to walk. Not just to get a man's attention. She just wanted the total self-confidence that Gloria seemed to have. She had not been there when they gave that out.

Today they were meeting for lunch again. How could it be? She, a little nobody from Podunk Junction, was now the Queen of Sweetwater's friend. Oh well, it had happened. Why? She just puzzled about that.

"Want a menu, ladies, or do you know what you want?" Jacqueline, her name tag said, wore two very long braids pulled up in the required net so it gave her a matahari look, especially when she added the net-looking hose. The Calla Lilly sported a waitress today. Sometimes Herb had to do it all. He had put in a deli and a blackboard menu, big as a school one to try to take out the need for extra help but he just couldn't cook, wash dishes, and wait tables. He knew how to cook well, just not how to run his business.

"A menu, absolutely. I don't have any idea what I want." When Jackie turned to go get them, Gloria said behind her hand, "She doesn't even want to work when she shows up, "and rolled her eyes at the ceiling. Lillie pursed her lips, knowingly.

Jacqueline glanced back at Gloria suspiciously. "Yes? Sweetie?"

"Nothing. You haven't given me the list yet, and I'm not your sweetie!. I mean would you want me to call you Jackie without asking?"

"I reckon not "came out so quietly Lillie barely heard the girl.

Herb was cooking burgers at the grill with his back turned to them. He glanced around, looking a little helpless.

Gloria noticed and took a deep breath. She took the menu Jacqueline offered.

"Look, I'm sorry, Jacqueline; I've had a very bad morning. Let's start over."

Lillie pretended to be picking something off the menu. She felt color rising to her own face.

Gloria's perfectly manicured long scarlet nail stopped on line five.

"Corned beef on rye sounds great if its available. And a large iced tea. Does a pickle and chips come with it.?"

"Sure, if you want. Kosher dill o.k.?"

"Perfect." Gloria was actually smiling now.

"Make that two; I've never had corn beef, I'll try it, "Lillie spoke up.

Over at table one Herb was delivering two Bubba Boy burgers. Mason the owner of Pickens Hardware was offering Herb free advice.

"Herb, you could use paper plates. Nobody would care. Save paying a dishwasher. Or, otherwise, you could marry some nice girl who would help you run this place. She'd be free."

Clyde, his son, asked "How you figure free, Dad? Next you'll be trying to tell Herb how to cook. Please don't do that. You can't."

Herb looked at Gloria and Lillie and shook his head. "Do you see what I have to put up with?"

"Surely do, Herb. You ought to charge Mason double.!" Gloria laughed.

"Hear, hear!" Clyde guffawed.

"I tell you, Herb, give the check to my boy here. He's feeling so big."

Lillie noticed Gloria looked tired.

"I'm sorry you had a rough morning. Tough customer?'

"Thanks, just tough hours, same as when Dad was alive. Dad wouldn't observe a strict 9-5day. If we had been a big funeral home, it would have been different. He thought anytime someone wanted to come was o.k. And we didn't do shifts. He wanted me there anytime he was unless I was sick. I told him we could discuss doing regular business hours like anybody else. He had this big comment then," 'Death is not by appointment, Gloria."

"I take my hat, which I don't wear, off to you, Gloria. I don't know how you do such a hard job. You must have a backbone made of steel."

"Think about it, Lillie. I'm in control. They don't talk back to me. Or argue with me. I make them look beautiful or at least nice, sometimes when they didn't in real life.

And families appreciate what you do. It's hard time in their lives."

"How did you ever get brave enough to work with the non-living?'

"It's o.k. to say dead, Lillie. I grew up in a funeral home with no mother and no brothers to say I shouldn't There was never really a question.'

"You didn't ever feel like rebelling or leaving town?'

"Not to leave my only kin, you know, my Dad. We disagreed, but I loved him."

Lillie nodded. Lillie's dad had left when she was five.

Chapter 56

THE INVESTIGATION

After the worst fire in Sweetwater's history, the town officials began an investigation into how the fire might have started. The facts that Briggs had a perfect delivery record, and one of their most beloved citizens had died in it drove the questions.

Abby kept recollecting how the mining company had objected to Dorrie and her endless questions. Billy agreed that they could not ignore that. The resentment he had first witnessed in Fulton's face at church was unforgettable. Fulton had addressed his answers to Galveston instead of answering Dorrie directly.

Ted had said to them that the boys had heard talk on the street by Sam Waters who was out of work that Dorrie was interfering with the progress of the town. Some of the store owners in Sweetwater felt the mining company might move on if there were too many objections and that would hurt their pockets. Others noticed that a lot of people had moved into town to work for the phosphate company, and others like Herb had started new businesses to serve the larger population. Sweetwater had grown from 1200 to 2000 people in a matter of months after the mining company had moved there. That was on the books

"You can understand their feelings if you've ever been out of work," he'd shared one night at the dinner table. Ted had. He himself had advised Dorrie that she should let the officials of the town decide about things. He was a little intimidated by Dorrie's remarks, thinking they should have been made by a man. But he did know they came from a good heart.

Some men in the Ruritan Club had said behind the closed doors of a Monday night meeting that the catastrophe hadn't happened until Donald had come back to town.

And now he was working for the phosphate company of all people. And they surely wanted to shut Dorrie up.

Look what Donald had to gain, one man said. No doubt he'd be the first named in his father's will with Dorrie gone. They knew Billy wouldn't put Ollie in charge of the strawberry farm. She just did not have the business sense. And look at how Billy's land sat side by side with the mining company's land? Would Donald leave it that way if the farm became his? If he got a good offer from Allgreen's for his father's land would he even stay here?

And so the rumor mill got started. Had Briggs been a pawn to help the fire along, someone asked? His health hadn't been too good. Maybe he'd started worrying about his retirement not being enough and become someone else's hit man.

It was true the phosphate company had the money to hire someone so their hands didn't have to do the dirty work.

But then Josh Rhine, an employee in the hardware store said that the day of the fire he had seen a stranger in town, matched whom Briggs had described, someone with a beard and hat and suit, a business-type of person. Who would that have been?

The longer the investigation went on, the more people divided on the subject. I'll will arose toward Donald which he felt when he went to the town to shop or do business.

Lillie volunteered that she thought it was just a terrible freak accident.

Who could have possibly been in Briggs' situation, witnessed a car drive into the telephone pole in front of him and the driver having a heart attack without responding to it? She felt they should not be criticizing or blaming Briggs for what would be considered an heroic effort under any other circumstances.

Some of the miners unhappy over the possibility of the phosphate company being made to move said it might have been someone from another town who wanted their town to have the money that was to be made from the mining of phosphate. After all, most small towns around were feeling a financial crunch and some jealousy. To other folks that sounded like a weak reason to commit manslaughter or murder.

It wasn't long before an accumulation of ideas from the Sweetwater community had reached Sheriff Robeson's ears. He decided he needed to think of a way to canvass all of the thinking on this matter.

Chapter 57

TOWN MEETING

Town meetings weren't held on any regular basis in Sweetwater. When someone thought there was a need for one, it might happen The last two were over adding another fire truck and a new water tower. The one before that was called by some of the ladies in town who wanted volunteers to help them beautify Main Street with some large geranium and petunia boxes. That gathering accomplished a lot. The sidewalk boxes were so pretty that Fred Gentry and Seth Applewhite transplanted some varieties of small maple and oak trees successfully and the town saw that a lot could be done if they worked together toward a goal.

In this instance, Sheriff Robeson felt he needed the collective benefit of any ideas or observations his friends had about Dorrie's death and the fire. He didn't know whether there were feelings that the fire might have been started on purpose or not. He had heard some rumors that suggested it might have been. That it might not have been a simple accident. He wasn't sure that is was good to do a collective investigation like this, but why couldn't it work in a small town? Jay Hobby the general practitioner agreed.

"You can do more intense work on your own, but some really helpful ideas could come out of it. Plus, these people need to talk about their hurt and loss."

So, the meeting was called on a Monday night. That way it didn't conflict with the Ruritan Club or the Garden Club on Tuesday or Wednesday night church meetings or Thursday night choir practices. They knew attendance wouldn't be good on a Friday.

From his seat on the front row Galveston looked around and knew he still saw anger in people's faces about Dorrie's death. It wouldn't do any harm for them to talk about it. He had frequently seen members who would be helped so much by his just listening to them. Maybe this meeting could help the town that way.

Walt Chaney was anxious to speak.

"Why didn't Briggs just call emergency? Didn't he realize when he went to that stranger's aid that leaving his post could result in a fire burning the whole town down?" Chaney asked the question some had been thinking but wouldn't voice.

"Right, Ed Tucker agreed. "What if the oil truck had exploded? It could have caught all the buildings downtown on fire."

"No, probably just the ones on that block." The newspaper editor spoke up.

"Well, that leaves your newspaper office out, doesn't it?" Chaney hurled back.

"Order now; request permission to speak." Robeson saw tempers flaring.

"I think if you'd seen the car jam into the telephone pole in the front of you and a man fall over inside, it would have gotten your attention, too."

A woman was angered by their attack on Briggs. "After all, Briggs isn't here to defend himself."

"But you could have cut off the fuel first, then gone to see about the man in the car."

"Yeah, if you'd had time to think through everything first. You don't have that kind of time in an emergency.

"It's like a reflex reaction in an emergency. You don't take time to think too long or you may lose the person." Galveston felt obligated to speak.

"But in this case, we lost one person, Dorrie, and actually it looks like Cliff Turner won't make it either. His son's going to make it but he'll have burned hands to deal with."

"I heard they had to do skin grafts on both hands."

"Did anyone have anything against Turner? Another idea.

"Are you crazy, a man in a wheelchair who would never have hurt a flea?"

"And worked hard every day of his life?"

Boy, Robeson thought, I sure opened Pandora's box.

"I request to speak." Robeson saw a hand raised.

"Granted."

"I think the question should be asked as it is always in situations like this, who would stand to benefit from Dorrie dying or Turner? I'm not making any accusations. I just think the question should be asked. Abby and Billy aren't here. Neither is Turner's son."

"Well, Turner's son is obviously a hero. That lets him out."

"Not necessarily. Haven't you ever seen those television shows that have the villain putting himself in danger to prevent suspicion?"

"Oh brother, is that far-fetched!" Somebody commented.

"So this means that we don't know at this point who was the target if there even was one?" Chaney was fast becoming the lead speaker, or instigator. Oh, well, Robeson reckoned. Chaney would sure keep things moving.

Robeson had to admit he hadn't really entertained the idea of Turner being target. The man had always been scrupulously honest.

"Well, look at Billy's strawberry farm? Who stands to inherit it?'

"Billy's still living; so is Abby. Wouldn't they have been the targets?"

"Well, they're getting older and Donald's back in town. You know they wouldn't leave the management of that strawberry farm to Ollie. She wouldn't be able to do it."

"And Donald's working for Allgreen's too. I heard Allgreen's would probably love to have Billy and Abby's farm, it bein' next to the phosphate company and all."

Chapter 58

BILLY'S WISHES

Billy stretched out in bed beside Abby and let out a big sigh.

"Are you tired, dear?"

"No, Abby, I was just thinkin' it's good after what's happened to have the other two children living on either side of us…"

"Well, I wouldn't get too used to it."

"Why do you say that, honey?" He turned to look at her, now frowning.

"Well Ollie's beginning to question what I say and do."

"Abby, she's an adult now, and she's been other places and lived. Maybe now she's home to stay."

"Mmm, I look at it like she already left twice before."

"Then I hope she finds a reason to stay this time."

"Billy, we won't always be here. A good man could look after her."

"The way the other two did?"

"Billy, they couldn't help dying."

"That's why I wonder if she'll marry again."

"Billy, I'd rather she marry than just carry on with someone. You know what I mean." Abby put her arm under her head.

"Not exactly…"

"Come on now. You know she's always liked attention from men."

"Don't most women?"

"Billy, you remember how she was in high school. Don't act ignorant!"

"O.K., I remember, but Ollie is beautiful and sweet. That was kind of natural."

"Billy, how many times did I slip out the screen door?"

"I don't know, Abby. How many times did you?" He smiled to himself.

"Billy, you know I had a perfect reputation!" She gave him a punch in the arm.

"Ow! That smarted!"

"But, Donald, he's a puzzle. Do you think he's content?"

"Oh, God, I hope, I wish." Billy rolled his eyes up and shut them tight.

"I know you do, Billy." She took his hand in hers to comfort him. But she was frowning and she wasn't sure why.

Chapter 59

THE RECKONING

Donald was in another morose mood. He had not been able to reach Gloria for three days. At this moment he had driven up from his house to hers, hoping to catch her there. He pulled his car into the boxwood-bordered driveway of the stately funeral home. Well, not promising. There was no visible signs of her. Wait, he saw the sleek black Buick in the garage as he pulled lower down into the drive. What was it doing here? Maybe she was out with someone. Who? It better not be another man. Was that why he hadn't been able to get her? Donald felt himself begin sweating as he got out of his car, crossed the unpaved dirt under the huge oak and climbed the back steps. His body was reacting just like when his wife had left him or when he had to go to big real estate meetings. The therapist had told him it was control issues or separation anxiety. He wiped the wetness from his forehead on his shirt sleeve before he knocked. His armpits had drenched his shirt so fast he felt like he had just stepped out of the shower. Confound it! This always happened to him at the worst times.

When Gloria's father died, he had urged her to move from here. This was such a forsaken-looking place since the small dynamic man was gone. He used to appear at any moment, keeping you on your guard. But then he could put you at ease with his golden welcome.

Donald wished he could have gotten to know him better. He felt they had been short-changed of a possible relationship. That is, if he and Gloria were lucky enough to have one. He'd begun to wonder lately.

He knocked again. No answer. There was no voice saying, "Just a minute, honey." God, he longed for that.

He tried the door. Locked. She wouldn't leave here without locking up. Such an old-fashioned lock. A skeleton key would open this. He fished in his pocket for the one from his back door. No luck. He felt all around the top of the door molding for it. Then his eyes fell to the bottom of the kitchen window to the left of the door. It was raised about four inches. The big screen in front of it. It was hooked? No! Yea! God was on his side. He pulled the screen out and turning his palms up, he pushed his fingers under the window. He used all his muscle, and it rose up above his head quickly. Ducking his body under it to crawl in, he didn't ask himself what he'd just done until he was inside. Boy, this would make Gloria furious, but suddenly he realized he'd have to take the risk. He had to see her. He sat down in the kitchen chair to wait for her.

Gloria watched Lillie drive away and turned forlornly toward the front steps. She didn't take time to go to the flagstone walkaway but went straight through the grass as if it weren't there. She didn't pay attention to the mud that collected on her shoe heels but tracked it up the steps to the huge front door. She fumbled in her shoulder bag for the thick key, then noticed her dirty shoes and kicked them off. Her chest hurt and she wished so much in her heart that her Dad was still inside to call out her name and scold her for the mud on the front porch. She listened once she was inside to the stillness, the hollowness of the front rooms. She took hold of the front banister to the stairway to pull herself up. She'd go upstairs. Maybe she could sleep.

"Gloria...She stopped in her tracks. She'd hear her name. From the back of the house. Somebody spoke. No. She was imagining again. She did a lot of that lately. Right now she'd welcome a ghost. She'd go get a glass of milk to carry up with her. She walked down the gloomy hallway and touched each table she passed outside both receiving rooms. Just as she reached the kitchen door she froze in her tracks. She was looking at the back of a man in a kitchen chair. He turned. She froze, then shrieked.

"Donald! What are you doing here? You scared me to death!"

But then suddenly he stood, staring at her, and she was in his arms, and he was smiling and crying over her smooth hair. She was holding him so tightly he could hardly breathe.

"Gloria, Gloria, you have such a pretty name!"

"Donald, Donald, Oh, Donald! I'm so glad you are here!" And she was repeating his name over and over again into his chest, and he looked down to see tears on her cheeks, too. Finally, he sat back down in the chair and took her on his lap. He laid his cheek on the top of her head and rocked her. For a long while they didn't say anything.

Chapter 60

DONALD AND GLORIA
AT CHURCH

She had cut a side look at Donald while Galveston had been preaching his sermon on commitment. In fact, several. He had just looked back at her and smiled...and wondered what she was thinking. He had told her he loved her. A man should tell a woman that a lot, shouldn't he?

He bet Galveston or Billy didn't. Of course, they were the good guys. They probably acted so good to their wives that the words weren't necessary. He wished he felt like he could be that way. What was different about him? Well, he'd been hurt by two women, that's what. His mother and his wife. What could be worse? How could he trust Gloria to be true to him? With her looks and business sense, she could probably have anyone she wanted. Oh, brother, he'd been on this page before.

Somebody had put peonies in the church today. They smelled so strong. They were flowers that really needed to stay in the yard. Gloria had insisted in sitting on the second row. If they had sat in the back, they wouldn't be smelling them. And the little kid who kept kicking his seat wouldn't be there if they were on the back row, would he?

The piano was pretty loud, too. Abby really got something out of banging those keys. She played the whole keyboard, no notes wasted.

"There is a fountain filled with blood"... that's a pretty gruesome image.

It that kid kicks this pew one more time...

Why does Gloria have on so much red today? I didn't think that was a church color. Maybe she's trying to attract other men.

That's it. I've got to go outside and take a smoke. I'm getting claustrophobic. If she'd just sat on the back row like I asked, I'd feel much better. Sitting here at the front you feel everybody's eyes on you. Boy, does that guy on the other side of Gloria need dandruff shampoo. She's looking ok at me. Hey, maybe she just thinks I'm going to the bathroom. I won't tell her about needing this cigarette. She'd just tell me I'm smoking too much if I can't wait one hour for another one.

Chapter 61

TRAVIS

"Criminy!"

Having said it, Travis had no idea what the word meant. How smart was that? He couldn't even curse right.

He reached down for his clipboard and pen which had tumbled to the floorboard of his car when he braked for the stoplight.

He was disorganized and such a fall-apart person he wondered every day how he had become a newspaper man. He was worse than a woman dropping stuff all the time, or was it a kid?

What was the matter with him?

After a couple of more sighs, he decided he better pull over and get lunch. His blood sugar might be getting lower. That's usually when he'd be down on himself the most or get confused. Good thing I'm a free-lance writer he thought. He gave himself enough criticism without a boss or supervisor to do it.

He was, after all, in a town he knew little about, but it was his destination. He was here to follow up on the Allgreen Phosphate Mining Company problems. They had certainly had some in Florida so he hopefully thought there would be some here. He signaled right off Main Street into the parking lot of the Calla Lilly Café, parking under a big oak. His was one of only five cars in the lot. Well, small town.

He was stiff from the long drive. He pulled up out of the low seat of the Toyota and stretched some. Too hot for his jacket so he shucked if off, tossing it into the back seat of the car. He rolled the long sleeves of his striped shirt up his forearms and removed his tie, sending it into the back seat as well. His beard felt a little warm, but he'd grown one because he got so tired of shaving. So make up your mind, old boy, he thought. Wanna go back to shaving in the morning? Not a chance, he thought.

He looked around what was probably the Main Street of Sweetwater. Not a bad-looking place. Flowers blooming in planters, benches where you could sit a spell, enough trees for shade. Storefronts and windows inviting enough. Dusty, though. Dry. He glanced down at his shoes. There was a powdery white dust mixed in with the usual tan dust. That surely looked familiar. Phosphate dust. Fossil shells crushed up fine in it.

On his way inside, he picked up a local newspaper from a rack, made his way to a booth. He always avoided tables out in the middle of the floor. That was where others could study you. He wanted to study them.

The owner, or cook, or both, looked his way and nodded to him.

"Jacqueline, you need to come help this gentleman who just came in."

"Alright, Herb, be right there."

In a moment she was. Fishnet stockings and all. A rather matihari look, black hairnet over braids on top of her head. Bright red lipstick. Some men would find her attractive. If he were her boss, he'd tell her nicely to lose the fishnets.

"Yes, sir, what can I get you to drink?"

"Sweet iced tea with lemon in either your biggest cup or a pitcher on the table."

"Gotcha, be right back."

No, you don't got me, not a chance, he thought. I wouldn't be able to turn my back on you. You'd be scouting another man.

She was right back. He had to give her that.

She sat the pitcher down on the table and recovered her order pad from her pocket.

"Now, the menu on the blackboard, did I tell you that? So what may I get you?"

"I think chicken salad, squash with onions, and green beans, thank you. No bread. No, you didn't tell me, but that's alright. I noticed the chalkboard at the front."

"Oh, sorry. You'll like the chicken salad. Herb puts grapes and nuts in it." She smiled but didn't linger.

She saved that for when she brought his ticket.

"You're new in town, aren't you? Her left hand rested on her hip. High heels.

"Well, yes, but I'm just visiting, thanks."

Over at the register, he noticed Herb cut down the grill. Then he walked over to Travis' table. This must be close to a one man show.

"Was the food to your liking?" First eye contact. Herb had kind, brown ones.

"It was delicious. I'll be sure to be back."

"Well, that's good." Herb smiled for the first time and handed him his change.

"Say, can you recommend a place to stay in town? I need one for a spell."

"Cottonwood Inn's where I suggest. Mary McNeill's the owner. Here's a little card with a map. You get supper with her rooms. Good cook, too."

"Well, thanks a lot. Hey, you ever thought of a show with Mata Hari there? You could do theater and charge double."

Herb laughed, "I don't know much about theater. My talent's in the kitchen, not on the stage."

"Well, the actors would be hard put to cook, probably. That is just what might make a good match. And give the town folks a place to eat and play, or just watch a singer or danger. Does Mata Hari sing?"

Herb raised an eyebrow.

"Actually, I think she might. She's in a Little Theater group. Come back and let's talk about what you know. Dinner'll be on me that time."

"You got a deal, Herb."

How about that? Travis asked himself as he crawled back under the wheel of the little Toyota. He pulled out the map to the Cottonwood Inn Herb had given him. Since he was on Main Street already, it looked like he could just take a right from the parking lot here and keep going until he ran into the street called "Low Fence." Wonder where that name came from, he thought. He bet Mary McNeil knew.

Chapter 62

TRAVIS MEETS MARY

"Everybody asks me that. Maybe that's why I suggested it. 'Low Fence.' It's an icebreaker. Every time." She pushed her sweater sleeves up her arms and sat down on the stool behind the inn desk. "Just like people ask if there are cotton mouth snakes around since this is the Cottonwood Inn. And there aren't that variety; just so you know."

"Mmm, "Travis also bet there was no lack of conversation with Mary around and he'd just met her. But that was good. He liked learning people and places. And that was one way you did it.

"Low Fence means we don't keep people or animals out. I like both. I saw the name High Gate on a street on a television show once and thought why would you want to name a street that?"

"I see your point," Travis said. That was all he had time to say.

"It sounds snobbish, don't you thing?"

"I certainly do," he agreed. He sat his suitcases down. He was liking the way Mary's friendly brown eyes caught the rays of the sun getting low through the screen door. The woman exuded warmth. Wonder if she had children?

"I'm sorry I'm just rattling on. Would you like a glass of tea or a cup of coffee? I have some in the kitchen. Also, supper's at six if you're interested.

"Thanks, Mary. A glass of tea would be great."

"I'll show you the way." When she smiled, long dimples appeared. Watching her move in front of him down the hall Clive thought if she lost weight she'd really attract some male attention. Particularly with the long black hair down that she currently had up in a loose bun. She'd told him briefly about the ex-husband who left with the money in the drawer. That would have been a dark time for her. Maybe she got through it by talking.

"Here's the kitchen." She glanced around at him. "Lord, you're still carrying your suitcase. I never told you which room, did I? I'd forget my head if it weren't attached."

When he walked through the doorway, Travis sat it down by the oil-clothed covered table and held up his right hand as if to stop her apology.

"That's o.k. , Mary. I'm not a greatly organized person either. You make me feel at home." His eyes went to the sink where a young woman stood washing pots.

"Supper's ready, Mary. I can show him where the room you want him to have is."

Was that correct English?" She dried her hands on the smocked apron.

"You're asking me? Lord, child, I never graduated."

The slender woman moved toward Travis and extended her hand.

"I'm Sahara, I live here with Mary." What astounding blue-gray eyes she had, Travis thought. Her hair was tumbling thick curls, unruly, but soft-looking.

"She's my right arm, she is." Mary beamed.

"Why don't you give him the room beside yours, Sahara? Key's on the hook at the desk."

Mary handed him the tea she'd poured, adding a slice of lemon to the top.

"Take it to your room, Travis. You can just bring it back to refill it for supper."

"Thanks, Mary."

"Come on, Niles, let's go show Travis his room."

Travis looked around but saw no one. Was there a ghost? Then he heard a long slip sliding at floor level. Coming around the kitchen table was the biggest snake he'd ever seen.

"Holy smokes! My country 'tis of thee! What is that?" When he looked down, he found he was on top of the picnic table on his knees.

"I'm sorry! He's my pet rattlesnake. He's not poisonous. I forgot to tell you about him. Some people have a dog or cat. We have a snake. But he makes a good guard dog, doesn't he Mary?" Sahara stepped over her pet. "I'll take him to my room. Let's put on your collar, Niles." Travis watch as she bent, pulled a small dog collar from her pocket, and clicked it around Nile's neck, or something like a neck. Below his head anyway.

Niles hissed in aggravation.

"Whew, if I hadn't seen it, I wouldn't believe it!" Travis whispered breathlessly.

"I apologize for not telling you about him," Mary said, "Out of sight, out of mind.

You'll make friends."

"I bet he is g –g-g-good watch dog." Travis observed, still from the table top.

I just don't think I want to make friends with a s- s –s- snake who wears a dog collar."

"You'd rather I took it off?" Sahara giggled

Chapter 63

TRAVIS UNDER OBSERVATION

"Girls, will you please notice the back booth. Either there's a new man in town or I need new glasses." Gloria rolled her dark brown eyes sideways at Lillie.

"You don't wear glasses, silly. You probably wouldn't wear them even if the doctor said you should, but you are right. I haven't seen him before." Lillie was smiling behind her napkin. She laid her fork down on the plate of half-eaten chef salad.

"Where does he come from, wonder?" Ollie asked her question of Lillie, Gloria, and Mary. "He doesn't look like anyone from around here."

"How much is the total answer worth to you all?" Mary smiled secretively and raised her eyebrows.

"Mary! You knew about him and didn't tell us?" Lillie sounded as if she couldn't believe it.

"He just got here yesterday. I was going to tell y'all today. He's a newspaper man." Her eyebrows were working again, once, up and down slowly.

"A newspaper man. Here in Sweetwater? Whatever for?" Gloria fingered her glass.

"Hands off, Gloria; you have Donald." Ollie pointed her finger at her friend.

"Honey, nobody has me. I'm not married yet." Gloria took a long draw from her straw.

"Oh, but y'all have been dating a lot, right?" Ollie asked.

"Oh, yes. He's been very attentive." Gloria admitted. "I have no complaints. It's just nice to have someone new to talk about. Sweetwater is suddenly growing."

"Is he staying at the Cottonwood, Mary?" Ollie looked back at the man in the back booth. He was really deep into the paper he was reading. She squinted.

"The Tampa News?" She said aloud.

"Tampa is where he's from." Mary was delighted to have the information her friends wanted.

"You're joking! What would he come here for?" Lillie frowned.

Herb startled her then by being at her elbow, pouring tea into her empty glass.

"You girls want me to introduce him to you?"

"Herb, you weren't supposed to hear that!" Lillie blushed and handed him the empty lemon dish.

"Tampa's mining phosphate, too, is what it's about."

"Phosphate, that's it." Mary confirmed Herb's statement and wiped her hands on her napkin.

"What else ya'll want to know about me?" Suddenly the man they'd all been discussing had pulled up a chair in the space beside Mary.

"Well, your name. A personal bio-sketch. But we weren't talking about you," Gloria lied, laughing.

"Well, let me introduce Travis from Tampa, ladies. I'll let him fill in the other blanks, though, or something in the kitchen will burn for sure." Herb hurried off.

"I'm Gloria; she's Lillie, and she's Ollie. I assume you know Mary since she told us about you. Whoops! I just let you know I lied, didn't I?" Gloria raised her eyebrows.

"You could say that," Travis smiled. "But it's reassuring to be notice by a table full of ladies, regardless. I have to admit that. Thank you."

All of them spoke of how Sweetwater was growing, of how new people had beg unto arrive, looking for work, or a change in their lives.

"That's how we came to know Lillie," Gloria reached to pat her friend's arm.

"Tell him about yourself, Lillie."

Then Gloria interrupted herself and pointed a well-polished red nail out the front window.

"Isn't that Sahara going into the fire department?"

Everyone agreed it was.

"That must be why she couldn't come with us tonight. But why did she have to go there?"

Mary said it before she remembered Lillie was on the other side of her.

"Getting back to phosphate," Travis threw in, and everybody but Lillie laughed.

Her attention was locked down the street on the front door of the fire department.

Chapter 64

VISIT TO THE FIREHOUSE

Sahara started out from Mary's fifteen minutes after Mary left the Cottonwood. Since the girls were having a girl's night out, tonight would be a good time to go see Chad. She supposed she could just call the firehouse to see if he were there, but the guys would brush off a non-emergency call. Sometimes when firemen weren't on a call, they washed the fire trucks, cooked or played with the dog. If she wasn't interrupting anything more important than that, he might talk to her.

As she left by the front walk, she smoothed her denim skirt down over her suntanned legs and pulled the lemon-colored tank shirt below her belt. She knew the yellow set off the highlights in her hair. If Chad wouldn't notice her, one of the others might.

It took her fifteen minutes to walk to the Main Street location. Maybe she'd check into a bike. She'd be getting a paycheck soon.

Chad was outside washing off the driveway. She noticed a "Safe Haven" sign in front of the station. What did that mean? If you were in some kind of danger, you could come here?

"Don't you want to ask me if I need some help, Chad?"

She flashed a winning smile.

"Truthfully, you don't look like you need any," Chad ventured.

"Well, if you don't know my name, you could ask." Sahara raised her eyebrows.

"Well, I have seen you somewhere before. Were you at church?"

She pursed her lips. "Well, yes; I spoke there."

"I'm sorry, I must have missed that Sunday."

"But, that's where we meet new people when they come to town, usually, unless at the drugstore or grocery or hardware."

"Wow, what are you telling me? That you aren't interested in a girl unless you meet her at church?"

"Oh, no, I'm sorry. I reckon that's what it sounded like."

"Well, you still haven't asked my name."

"Usually somebody is supposed to introduce you to a girl, right, for it to be proper?"

"Well, call one of your friends out here," Sahara advised him.

"No, that's o.k.. What is your uh, uh name?"

Why he's shy, very shy, Sahara thought

"It's Sahara."

"That's a pretty name. Unusual."

"Do you want to know where I live?"

"Sure, where's that?"

"Mary McNeil's. You know, the Cottonwood Inn."

"Oh, yeah, she's a real nice lady."

"Oh, yes, she's given me a job. I told her she ought to make the Inn into a rooming house to make more money. That way folks moving to town could room there, maybe."

"Well, with all the new people at the mining company, that just might work.

Good idea, Savannah." Chad hung the hose back on its rack and turned to her.

"It's Sahara, Chad." I made a real impression, Sahara thought.

"Hey, Chad, chow's on. Hey, who's your new friend?

"Don't mind him, he's a flirt." Chad said, but as he spoke, he noticed she was looking with interest at his six-foot fellow fireman, Greg, who was standing in the doorway.

159

Chapter 65

THE CONFRONTATION

Mary finally stopped folding the tablecloth and addressed Sahara's back. They were in the kitchen. Sahara was working on lunch at the sink

"Sahara, what were you doing at the Fire Department last night?"

"What do you mean?" Sahara was put off-guard by the question.

"Well, in that my good friend Lillie saw you, and I'm sure she wondered." Mary wasn't backing down.

"Aren't I your good friend, too?" Sahara sounded threatened.

"Of course you are. You're like a sister I never had. That's why I asked."

"Oh…well." Sahara looked down.

"It wouldn't be Chad, would it? Sahara turned to see Mary looking straight at her.

"Couldn't it be, Mary?" Sahara's voice sounded like a wistful child to Mary.

"Sure. Sahara, if you want to break Lillie's heart."

It became very quiet. Sahara turned back to put the paring knife she'd been using on the carrots down on the drain board. Her hands gripped the sink until her knuckles turned white.

"Did he invite you over?"

"No, I didn't know ya'll would be at Herb's. I went over to try to see Chad."

"Well, that's honest enough."

"Mary, I wouldn't hurt Lillie on purpose."

"You just might without thinking?"

"You needn't worry. He must like Lillie. He didn't even get my name right. But Greg did. He asked me out. So, don't worry. I'm going to go out with Greg."

She looked at Mary and crossed her heart.

Mary stepped forward and took Sahara's hands.

"I'm very glad, girl. Now is there anything I should ask you about this young man, Sahara, before you go out with him? Is Greg nice, hardworking...?"

Sahara reached forward to hug Mary. "Thank you for caring, Mary. My mother wasn't around to show me that."

Chapter 66

MISSING

Travis stood on the steps wondering if he had forgotten something about the conversation. He was early. He had knocked on the door of Ollie's trailer three times now, and she hadn't answered it. He hesitated, then opened the screen. When he did, the front door swung open. It was unlatched? He walked in and stood in the half-light of the small living room. All was quiet. The kitchen on the other side of the bar counter was empty.

"Ollie… Ollie?

He had told her he would be here at eight. They were going to discuss the mining issues, but as he looked around he saw the blinds were still not raised. He finally walked down the narrow hallway, calling her name. When he came to what must be her bedroom door, he paused. Yes, there it was, her bed, pink-flowered comforter pushed back, pink sheets rumpled, and at the window, blue ruffled curtains with tiebacks. There was no water running as if she were bathing. The bathroom door was open. He glanced in and noticed a toothbrush lay on the counter beside the open tube of toothpaste.

There were no early morning smells of coffee as he walked back up the hall. No hint of bacon or sausage aroma in that space. He looked in the sink. There was no cereal bowl. And the most disturbing thing.

Her brown pocketbook sat in the living room chair. That would have to be the one she was using.

The signs were there that her bed had been slept in. But she was not here. Where was she this early in the morning that she hadn't taken her pocketbook? Of course. That was it. She must be at her folk's house next door. He turned to go back out through her front door, and when he stepped out, he almost stepped on a large, ginger-colored cat who meowed at him.

"Hey, kitty, where is Ollie? You wish you knew, too?"

He noticed the empty food bowl. Usually people fed their pets in the morning, didn't they? He didn't know. He didn't have one.

As he started to cross the yard to Abby and Billy's a cry startled him. It came from the back yard. He heard it again. It was a woman's voice.

"No, Billy, I can't take it! I can't take anything else. Oh God, please."

He started running toward the sound and called out to them as he rounded the house and saw them in the backyard.

"Mr. and Mrs. Fuller. I'm Travis, a friend of Ollie's. Is she here?"

The older couple looked at him in surprise.

"I've just checked at her trailer, and I thought she might be over here having breakfast with you all."

"Have we met, young fellow?" Billy looked puzzled.

"I'm sorry, I'm a reporter in Sweetwater about the mining issue. We haven't met, but I met Ollie with her friends at The Calla Lilly last night. Herb introduced us. Mary McNeill told me that Ollie and you might be some help with my story."

"Young man, whatever your name is, Ollie is missing! We haven't seen her this morning. We're very worried. She almost always has breakfast with us. But when I called she didn't answer, and I can't find her."

Then Abby covered her mouth with her hand as if saying what was on her mind was too terrifying.

"Now, now, Abby, she can't be far. Maybe she stepped down to Cora's or something. We'll find her." Billy tightened his arm around Abby.

"She can't be far. She left her pocketbook on the living room chair."

Travis said this matter- of- fact- like, but Abby looked suspiciously at him.

"How do you know?"

"Her door is open, or rather unlatched. I stepped inside after I knocked three times, and she didn't come to the door or call out."

"Could you…"

"Can you help us look for her?" The panic on Abby's face and in her voice stirred Travis. He remembered Herb talking about the fire that had killed Ollie's sister.

… that wouldn't be right!

"Sure, I don't have anything to do. I'll drive. Is there anybody else who should be called first?"

"I can't think of anyone, son. You're real kind to help us. Thank you."

Chapter 67

CONTACT

They first drove by Cora's to see if Ollie had gone there to help with Fred. Cora hadn't seen Ollie but was worried that they didn't know where she was. It was too early in the day for her to have been going anywhere, Cora observed, so she couldn't be far. Anyway she didn't drive so where could she have gone, except on foot?

That was what was bothering all of them secretly. Ollie didn't drive. So how far could she be on foot?

"Why isn't she still in her bed? She usually sleeps later than we do." Abby wasn't having any of her having gone out with a friend. After all, she never did that this early in the day.

Billy didn't know what to think except that she wasn't an early morning person. So Abby's thinking that none of this made sense, made sense.

Travis had just met Ollie last night so he had no basis for comparison. There was, however a newspaper reporter's foreboding building in his brain.

They really didn't know where to go next so Billy made a suggestion.

"If you don't mind, Travis, drive up to the store. Once in a long while she'll walk up there for something one of us needs."

"Sure, Billy."

At the store, Tillie Morgan said she'd seen Ollie.

"She was in here just for coffee and bananas. Said she woke up early and had no coffee and wanted bananas for her Cheerios."

"Was she by herself?" Abby knew Tillie would usually know everything that was going on with anybody. And shared it with you whether you asked or not.

Well, let's see. Sure, I know. Those Carson boys are hard to ignore. They bought cigarettes and beer, as usual. Made some crude remarks to Ollie. They always give her a hard time ever since she told them off that day in here. About Billy being silly about going into strawberry farming.

"I didn't know about that," Billy looked quizzical. "Why didn't somebody tell me they were giving her a hard time?"

"Oh, Billy, she really got them told that day, said if *they* weren't so lazy *they'd* know how to do something worthwhile. Something to that effect. Everybody liked seeing them get their comeuppance.

Uh, oh thought Travis to himself. She made some enemies that day.

"What out of line thing did they say to Ollie?' Abby wanted to know.

"How she shouldn't be unfriendly, that she obviously had worn out two husbands."

"You're kidding me. They talked that way to my Ollie?"

"Well, Abby, it may not be word for word, but it's close."

"Did they leave when Ollie did?" Travis had a knot in his throat.

"It was a little while after her." Tilly finished bagging the rice and bananas and lettuce Abby had brought.

"So they were the only people in the store when Ollie was." Travis was checking the facts.

"Yes, I'm sure of it, now. If anybody else had been in here with me, they wouldn't have gotten away with talking to Ollie like that. I'd have set them straight myself. I just didn't have anybody to back me up. They'd as soon smack someone as look at them. No respect. One of these days they're going to go too far and end up in the big house. I've heard a few people say it."

"Folks, let's hit the road, I think we should follow what way Ollie would go home. Do you know what way she'd walk?" Travis couldn't hide his worry anymore.

"There really isn't but one way, Travis. The way we came." Billy took the bag in one hand and Abby's hand in his other to hurry her.

"Thanks for your help, Tillie." Abby took a deep breath.

"Of course. You know I love Ollie. Let me know as soon as you find her."

Chapter 68

LOOKING FOR OLLIE

Billy witnessed Abby yank the sweater onto her arm so hard it pulled a hole in the shoulder when they left the store.

"Here, honey, you've got the sleeve inside out." He reached to pull it through for her. "Are you cold? It's probably 75 degrees out here."

"Bill, I'm no invalid. Leave this fool sweater be; it's old as the hills. Worry about what's important! Yes, I'm cold; I can't help it!" Abby opened the car door herself instead of letting Travis, slamming it harder than necessary. She climbed into the back seat but sat on the edge like a child might to see, holding onto the door handle so hard her fingers turned white.

Travis heard her mumble through her teeth something about those "blasted Carson brothers," that "they better not come in my sight when I'm holding my shot gun ! It might just accidentally go off."

"Just take it back the way we came, Travis. I've got no other idea, yet." Billy scrunched forward too, and had his right hand on the dash and his left hand on the top of the seat, turned toward Travis as they drove away from the store.

Travis heard Abby say "Those sorry so and sos. They ought to be horsewhipped for talkin' that way to my Ollie!" He agreed with her for sure but thought he never wanted to cross her.

Billy looked as if he wanted to see both where they were going and where they'd been at the same time. Travis could figure that.

"Travis, understand my wife's upset. Normally she puts all this passion mainly into her piano playing."

"Billy Fuller, you know better than to try to talk for me!'

"Sorry, honey, you're right." Billy raised his eyebrows but kept looking forward, Travis noticed.

"Folks, what about the girls she was with last night? What if one of them called? Wanted to eat breakfast, or something?" Travis hunted for some clue.

"It'd be mighty out of character," Abby muttered. "Of course, she's shown some independence of late." She was thinking of the arguments she and Ollie had had lately about the stuffed animals, about mud on the porch, and another about what she should wear to Dorrie's funeral.

"Yeah, she's been puttin' herself forward more. Course that's not a bad thing."

"Billy, what if it has gotten her in trouble! That'd be bad, wouldn't it?"

Travis saw Abby's mouth tighten into a grim straight line, like it was used to it.

"Standing up for herself will more likely make her stronger, Abby. We're getting older. We won't always be here."

"Thank you for reminding me I'm older! Let's just keep our eyes open. She's bound to be walking back or gotten home by now, don't ya'll think?"

"Are there any turns off this road?" Travis wished they had overlooked something. He scanned first one side, then another, looking for any sign of her.

"No, you should slow down near Little Creek, though. She just might stop near the bridge to watch the fish."

169

I hope not unless it was out of sight of those Carson brothers, thought Travis. You would think I knew her better the way my stomach is all knotted up. This was the longest two-mile ride he'd ever been on.

Billy eased his body back against the seat finally. He reached up to hold on to the door strap with his right hand.

"Hey, look, whoose truck is that? That green one?" Travis applied the brake some.

"I don't know; it looks familiar, though." Billy scratched his head with his other hand.

"Where you think the driver is?"

"Probably huntin' or gone to use a tree."

"Let's move on. There's nobody in it. I think she's going to have beat us home."

Abby was still sitting on the edge of the seat.

But when they got to the house, everything was like they left it. No sign of her. They walked resignedly into the kitchen. Billy poured three cups of coffee without asking them. He took the phone from the hook and opened the little book of numbers.

Chapter 69

THE CARSON REVENGE

She was relishing the walk from the store. It gave her a chance to think, and she always loved seeing the animals. Today, she sauntered along kicking a pine cone ahead of her, swinging her bag. She finally realized, though, that the steady looking down was giving her a crick in her neck so she glanced up to rest it. She studied one of the cotton-candy-like clouds at the horizon and saw that it looked like an elephant's head with floppy ears and trunk. A run-on melody interrupted her animal study. It came from high above her and stopped her in her tracks. A mockingbird serenaded her, trilling from one song into another. She looked for the tallest branch around where she finally spotted him. He looked sassy and proud of his song for her, switching his black and gray stand-up tail feathers.

"Hey, nice concert!" she called out.

On her last walk to town she had just about stumbled headlong into a mother possum meandering across the road followed by all the little ones. She had been lost in her thoughts, wondering how she could handle Mama and all her attempts to change her. She had wished she could scoot the possum along without scaring her. If she didn't hurry, she'd get hit. They came out at night, so why was she out during the day? And then she had heard the heavy machinery in the distance at the mine. .

It was chilly out here today in this wind. She wished she had remembered to wear a scarf. It would have helped manage her long hair that kept whipping in the sharp breeze. She fingered the long, turquoise blue berets she had pulled the sides up with this morning. Dorrie had given them to her, and although Mama had never criticized Dorrie for anything, she told Ollie she shouldn't wear things that called attention to herself. Why didn't Mama get tired of drab colors? Ted had offered if she would be happier he would get a friend of his to move her trailer onto the lot next to him and the boys. He said she'd be bound to have more freedom. As it was, she felt Mama's watchful eye over everything she did. And because her trailer was on their land she felt she needed Mama's approval for any plan she made, like having someone over. And she worried now about moving away. So she didn't ask.

She felt so by herself today. She'd lost two kind husbands and her best friend and sister, Dorrie. She stopped at the Little Creek Bridge. She leaned over the wooden railing trying to spot the bass or brim she liked to watch swim around. Today she noticed the water was not flowing like usual. It looked brackish cloudy grey. She couldn't even spot any fish. Boy, that was disappointing.

Gosh, she missed Dorrie. Dorrie never made fun of her love of animals. Mama said she reckoned she should have sent Ollie huntin' or fishin' with the boys when she was growing up. That was how much Mama understood. Ollie had never wanted to kill an animal or a fish. She liked to watch them move or play. Ted had asked her if she would like an aquarium. She told him she doubted that. She liked to watch them swim free.

She looked up when she heard some noise up the road. It was a truck. She had about another mile and she'd be home. Dust swirled up from the tires as they swiped the shoulder in someone's hurry. Suddenly, it stopped beside her.

"Want a ride home, Ollie?"

She knew the voice. It was Earl Carson, but she knew Ralph was with him. He always was.

"No, I like to walk." Why would she possibly want a ride with them?

"Well, looky here, we'll be good neighbors since you don't drive. Come on.

We'll take you home."

Could they be serious?

"No, that's alright." She didn't trust either one of them.

"Well, that's not very neighborly, is it, to refuse a kindness offered?"

'No, it isn't, "Ralph answered his brother.

"Sure isn't."

Before she knew it, they had gotten down out of the truck and were snickering, coming toward her.

"You've got a stupid Papa, Ollie. Know what makes you?"

She felt smoke trying to come from her head. They were trying to make her fight them. Keep calm, that's what Dorrie always told her. You can't think with a hot head!

She tried to run from them, but two were too many for her to handle. The quickly picked her up under each of her arms and carried her forward into the woods.

"Turn me loose; I'll scream!" Ollie threatened.

"Who's gonna hear you?" They jeered.

There was no escaping what they wanted. Later, when she finally realized they were speaking about going, she heard Earl hiss at Ralph through her pain.

"Hey, look, her bills fell out of her pockets; let's get her money, too!" She had her eyes shut from the sight of them, but she felt them pawing at the ground on either side of her, and she squinted and reached beside her to grab fistfuls of the sandy soil and hurl it up into their eyes.

"What the…! You blinded me! Ralph Help!" Earl yelled. She heard the truck keys hit the ground and saw Earl rake his hands across his eyes.

"Oh, no…! I can't see! Earl" Ralph screamed back. "She's blinded me!"

That's what Ollie counted on. She dove for the keys and rolled over and upward, adrenalin pushing her running toward the truck. In seconds, she scrambled up into the driver's seat.

Through the truck window, she could hear Earl and Ralph still screaming at each other in the woods.

"You idiot, Earl, you were driving! She's getting' away! Where are the keys?"

"I don't know! Don't you have yours?"

"No, stupid, I didn't need them. Remember, you were driving."

So, while Earl and Ralph argued and fought, knocking each other to the ground to prove their points, Ollie was praying aloud.

Lord, help me, she breathed. She jammed the key into the ignition like she'd seen Papa do and turned it. She pushed down on the pedal like she'd seen her father do. Then again. Then she heard the motor sputter, catch, then roar.

In a moment she'd left them in the dust. She had some problem steering the truck around the curves. One bridge looked so narrow to drive over that she almost slowed down. It seemed much further than the mile it must have been to the driveway to Papa's house. Finally, she saw it straight ahead, and she barreled across the intersection and right into Papa's driveway. She turned off the engine to stop the truck and reached down between the seats like she'd seen Papa do and pulled the emergency brake. Her heart pounded in her eardrums, and she couldn't catch her breath. She dropped forward on the steering wheel closing her eyes. Then she heard the horn blow.

Her arms hurt. She was holding on for dear life. She didn't want to see.

"Ollie, honey, look at me, what's the matter?"

She heard he father calling her name and felt his arm around her.

"Ollie! What in the world happened?" Her mother was pulling straw out of her hair and smoothing it.

She turned her wet face to them. "Call the sheriff. The Carson brothers…" Then she just shook her head and fainted when she moved down out of the truck and tried to stand up. Her knees buckled, but Travis caught her.

"Abby, you tell me where to put her. I can carry her inside. Billy, you call the sheriff. Whoever's truck that is may come to get it! We'll stop them until we find out what's happed to her!" He picked Ollie up like she might have been a child. Abby ran in right behind, ordering Travis to take her to their back bedroom. After Travis laid her down on Abby's bed quilt, he came out to let her mother look after her.

Back in the living room he saw Billy's mouth in a grim line now and noticed the truck keys lay on a table beside his chair.

"The sheriff's on his way That truck belongs to those no-good Carsons! Keep watch; I'm going to get my shotgun, 'case they get here 'fore he does!"

Chapter 70

AFTERMATH FOR ABBY

Ollie had barely told Abby anything about what happened with the Carsons. She had stopped because she had gotten a strange reaction. Abby had frowned at her, told her she shouldn't wear pink lipstick and shiny berets in her hair, and offered her no sympathy.

If Ollie had known the whole truth, she'd have been sadder. Abby had actually asked Billy did he remember how Ollie had liked attention from the boys in high school, and did Billy think she could have led them on?

Billy have been astonished at her question. "You'd believe those sorry so and so's over Ollie?"

"You know their reputation, and you're taking their word that Ollie invited them into the woods. I don't believe you!"

He'd even been so upset, he'd told her not to fix him any supper. That was a first.

He'd asked her had she even noticed that Ollie was smart to get the keys and drive the truck to their house?

Yes, she had. "That was amazing!" She wondered aloud, though, if Billy thought they'd charge Ollie with taking the truck.

"Woman, your daughter has been attacked, and you're wondering if they'll charge her with stealing the truck when what she was doing was escaping from them? I think God himself helped he get those keys to the truck. She was smart enough to know what to do from here."

"Really?" Abby pondered that. Billy was pretty angry sounding so she went to talk it over with Cora McGillicutty.

"How were they when they came to get their truck, Abby? They had to come to your yard to get it?"

"They tried to hot-wire it, Billy said because they didn't have any other keys."

""Well, that should tell you something. Why, if she'd invited them to the woods, would she not wait for them to bring her home, or let her off nearby."

"Maybe she was afraid after she got into it?"

"Abby, I think Billy is exactly right. They took advantage of her out on that isolated road. And they were extremely afraid of getting caught because they had to come to your house to get their truck. Think about it! She's 35 now, Abby. Not sixteen. She's been through two husbands' deaths."

"She's so fine-looking, though, Cora."

"Yes, she is. And you're here holding it against her instead of holding those two no-accounts to account for their actions. They've always been a jail-sentence waiting to happen."

Abby became silent. Cora had always been straight with her.

"Cora, don't you remember how she was in high school? She sneaked out of the house to meet Angus. Don't you remember?"

Cora shook her head. "I know, Abby, but that was because she was sixteen and you wouldn't let her date him openly."

"Well, she's made many mistakes in her life. I was just trying to protect her."

"Well, have you heard anything I've said?"

Abby was nonplussed. "I'm not a child, Cora."

"But you're refusing to listen to common sense, Abby. What I don't understand is why you choose to believe their story? You don't treat what Ollie says like this all the time, do you?"

Abby was quiet again.

"Well, I've got to go." Although, she didn't. Why was her chest hurting? She felt almost sick.

She took it slow walking home. When she got to the front yard, she thought where was Billy? His truck was gone. What Cora had said last kept echoing in her head.

There were some fried okra and turnip greens covered on the table. Some fat back Ollie had fried was on a plate on the stove. There was batter in a bowl. She must be planning cornbread for supper. Where was she?

She tiptoed down the hall. The door to the front bedroom was open. She looked in and saw Ollie lying on the bed in a robe. Her hair was wet. She'd had a shower, Abby thought, but had fallen asleep afterward. Her face showed she'd been crying.

Abby felt so ashamed. Ollie had managed to cook supper despite how she felt. Ollie was always trying to make them feel better Abby realized, thinking back. Ollie was actually a pretty good cook. Cora had told her one day she was lucky to have a daughter. Two, in fact.

Cora had no daughters or sons. Her husband had been disabled in the war. Cora looked after him now.

Abby felt tears coming to her eyes as she walked softly down the hall. She dabbed at her eyes with the bottom of her apron. She had been regarding a blessing in her life as a bother. What God must think of her. She suddenly saw in her daughter some of the things other people appreciated about her... her helpfulness, her kindness, her generosity. She felt deeply a conviction of sin... of taking Ollie for granted, of misjudging her good character. As she stood in front of the piano where a picture of all four of them sat, she realized the qualities she was recognizing now in Ollie were ones she learned from Dorrie, her sister, not from her.

And Ollie had driven the truck, to boot. Finally she shook her head in wonder about that.

Chapter 71

AFTERMATH FOR OLLIE

Ollie felt she'd never be clean again. She'd already had two showers today and it was just 1:00 p.m. Abby had asked her if anything was wrong, but she couldn't really talk about it. She couldn't clearly see the clothes she was folding from the backyard line. Her eyes were filling up again. She felt such rage inside. If there hadn't been two of them, she could have fought one off. She pulled a washcloth from the basket and dried her eyes. How could she ever look at people again? She felt so dirty. Why did she feel so guilty? It wasn't her fault it happened. She kept telling herself that. But if her own mother didn't believe her? Abby hadn't really said she didn't; Ollie just knew she didn't.

What if nobody believed her? Well, Papa did, she was sure. She saw it in his eyes. It was as if he figured what had happened to her before she told him. She hated the hurt she saw in his eyes. He didn't often talk about his feelings being hurt. Probably it was because he was a man.

What had she done to deserve this?

When she woke up later, she smelled supper cooking… pork chops cooking. She'd only meant to rest her eyes. The bedspread covering herself into the kitchen.

"I'm sorry, Mama. I was going to finish supper. I got some of it done. I just got tired and fell asleep."

She'd told them she could help them with cooking and other chores when she moved back. They didn't want her to pay for heat, lights, water. Her trailer was plugged into their house.

"I'm glad you did fall asleep."

"What?"

"I heard you cry out in your sleep last night so I know you didn't sleep well. I started to come in your room but you got quiet again."

Mama... sorry?

"I'm worried about you, Ollie. You haven't been yourself for days. If you can't talk to me about it, maybe you could talk to Cora or Galveston."

"Mama, it's hard to talk about. Awful..."

"I'm sure, girl. I'm, I'm very sorry I didn't believe you at first. Your father told me I was wrong, but you know how hard-headed I am."

Was this Mama?

"It's o.k., Mama."

"Well, I'm truly sorry, child."

"Mama, you said I could talk to you."

"Sure you can, girl."

Later, when Ollie had described in detail to her mother what had happened, Abby felt such heat rising in her chest.

Her daughter had been ravaged by those brutes. No question.

She held Ollie close to her for a long while and smoothed her hair.

"Ollie, you'll never have to walk that road again, child."

"What do you mean, Mama?"

"Because you drove the truck the other day in an emergency. I think we ought to get the driver's manual for you to study. Papa's always thought you could drive. Now I believe him. I'm just sorry it took so long."

For the first time in many days Ollie smiled.

"Thank you, Mama."

And when her mother pulled her to her to hug her, Ollie hugged her back.

Chapter 72

ADAM'S MOVE

Adam picked up the phone, then placed it back in its cradle. After the third time, he finally dialed Ollie's number. He had been meaning to make this call for a while now.

Ollie was headed out the door to eat fried chicken and collards at her Mom and Dad's. She smelled the aroma as she closed the screen door. It took her only three strides to take the phone off the wall in the kitchen.

"Yes,... yes,... well, o.k., I think so. Yes, I'd like to see the site. All right. Five-thirty, then, tomorrow."

Strange, she thought as she locked the door behind her. He's never even spoken to me in church before.

Adam Philyaw, head CEO of ALL-Green Phosphate Mining had just invited her to come for a personal tour of the company tomorrow. He wanted her to see the upcoming changes.

"Pop, hi," Ollie greeted her dad as she went in their back-screen door. Did you get a call from Mr. Philyaw today?"

"No, Ollie, sure didn't. I'd remember that."

"Philyaw? Is that what you said, Ollie?" Donald was already at the table with the paper. One-half a slice of cornbread sat on his plate with butter melting on the top.

"Yes, he called to see if I wanted to tour the mining company property tomorrow. He said since I'd been partly responsible for the changes they're making, he wanted me to see for myself."

"Well, now," Donald said, laying the paper down. "You got a call; Pop didn't. Wonder what that means?"

"Probably that he'd rather take a pretty young lady than an ugly old man," Billy guessed.

"He's married, though, Pop. Nobody's seen the wife in person. I hear she calls him at the office, though." Donald helped himself to the mashed potatoes. "Frequently."

"Maybe he's planning on calling you later, Pop." Ollie thought aloud.

"I doubt it. I don't see a no-nonsense man like Adam taking work home with him." Billy dug a spoon into the pole beans. Ollie took the plate of fried chicken from Abby.

"Mama, this food smells so good, it would make anyone want to sit right down and eat with us."

"You think so, Ollie? Don't fool me now." Abby smiled and was obviously pleased with the compliment.

Ollie remembered Lillie had told her a few sincere compliments she might pay her mother might pave the way for them to relate better.

"More flies are caught with honey than vinegar," Lillie had reminded her about the old saying.

Ollie notice her father smiled to himself and said "Amen, sister." Billy had been trying to help Abby with her grieving over Dorrie by getting her out of the house more. Lately he'd taken her to Herb's to eat or over to a movie in Bluffton, insisting she worked too hard as it was in the garden.

The day Ollie had known it might not hurt her to try helping her mother with her grief was the day her mother said she wanted to quit playing the piano for church. She'd never seen her mother that depressed before Dorrie died. She'd convinced Abby she was the onlymember in the church who could play well enough to accompany the choir. She'd also told Galveston what her mother had said.

"Let me know if he calls you to go, too, Dad." Donald sunk his front teeth into the tender chicken thigh.

"O.K., Donald, I will."

"Who do you want to tell you what, Donald?" Ollie snapped back from her thoughts.

"Boy, you were out on another planet, weren't you, sis, but then you often are, aren't you?"

Ollie picked up the paper and sweated him with it.

Chapter 73

DONALD'S MOVE

"Dad, did you ever get a call from Philyaw?" Donald called at noon the next day

"No, I didn't, Son, but I wasn't expecting it."

"Well, you could just ride with her."

"Well, I would, but Abby's got me helping her can this morning."

"Oh, O.K.. Dad, I'll talk to you later."

Donald hung up, still puzzling why Philyaw hadn't called his dad instead of Ollie. Billy was more of a figure in the community.

It wouldn't hurt anything he supposed to walk over to Adam's office when 5:00 came. To see where Adam was going with this. He'd better not be planning to hit on his sister. Although what red-blooded male wouldn't want to try?

At 4:45 p.m. Donald got a call from his immediate boss, Hurley, to report to him. For then he had to forget about checking on Ollie and hope for the best. After all, Ollie was getting more mouth these days. He just hoped Adam's plan wasn't to shut her up.

"Come on in, Donald," Hurley called out. "How are things with you?"

"As well as things can go under the circumstances, Hurley. Things still get tough for Mom about Dorrie. We all have bad days, even Pop."

"I'm sure, Donald. I'm so sorry about your loss. Dorrie was one fine person. She didn't deserve to die so early and the way she did."

"No. No one really deserves that. And she meant a lot to Sweetwater. A lot to this community."

"You're right. She believed in this little town. Wanted to make sure this mining company did the right thing. No one can argue with that."

"You're right." Donald thought. He wished he thought Adam agreed with that thinking.

"Well, here is a new job description Adam has written for your position, Donald. Take a look."

"It has grown a little, right?" Donald asked as he skimmed the paper.

"Yes, Adam said he wanted to kind of promote you."

"How much more money, Hurley?"

"That's not set. He plans a raise based on how the next three months goes."

"No incentive raise, Hurley?"

"No, not at first, Donald."

"Well, that doesn't seem as fair as it should be. Seems like the raise should be in place the first month on a true promotion." Donald frowned at the list.

"You want me to quote you on that, Donald?"

"Sure, Hurley, I'm willing to do more. I'd just like the pay to match the work I do."

"I'll tell him, Donald and get back to you."

Donald stepped out into the sun and spotted his father's truck. Well, he reckoned Billy came after all. No, wait a minute. Ollie had just gotten her license. So she probably drove. It was a good thing they sent those Carson boys away from here. There were a lot of folks angry about what had happened to Ollie.

He walked across the concrete yard to Adam's office. His secretary said he and Ollie had already toured the area where the lunchroom and showers were to be constructed. She stood and pointed out the window down below them in another direction.

"He said if she were interested he might take her on a tour of the pit itself."

"That's not real safe." Donald frowned to himself.

"I don't like it myself, either. It's loud and the machinery's heavy." The secretary observed.

"Did they wear hard hats?"

"I don't know, sir, I'm sorry."

Of course, Ollie would want to go see the actual mining, Donald mused. Just like her sister in that regard. She'd want to know where her nephews were actually working. Was it safe? After all, coal mining had never been a safe work environment. It was below ground level and without proper air circulation. That's the reason there were so many sick coal miners now and ones that hadn't lived past middle age.

Chapter 74

POSSIBILITIES

Gloria and Lillie had gone by to see if Sahara and Ollie wanted to go to a movie and dinner in Bluffon which was 30 miles away. To herself, Abby had entertained doubts about Ollie going but said nothing: there was safety in numbers after all. And, she thought, look at the business that Gloria had helped her Dad run all those years.

When Sahara and Ollie piled in the back seat of the funeral limousine, Gloria hollered to Mary.

"Mary, why don't you go with us? How long has it been since you went out to a movie?"

"I can't remember," Mary admitted. "But you younger girls need to get out together."

"Funny, I never thought of you as older. Look what you've done with the Inn by yourself. You didn't do that from a rocking chair."

Mary rolled her eyes to the right and pursed her lips. "Maybe you've got a point, Gloria, thank you."

"Exactly." Gloria gave a quick nod.

"Mary, go put on your flamingo shirt and slacks. We can wait, right, Gloria?"

Sahara was glad to see Gloria in something besides a suit.

"Sure, no hurry. We've got nobody saying when we have to be home. We're grown folks, right, ladies?"

There was a brief, startled silence before they all chorused "Yes!"

"Be right back." And Mary scurried back up the pine straw path faster than Sahara had ever seen her move.

When Mary returned she had applied some lipstick that matched her outfit, one she had told Sahara she had bought and "never worn but once." She said she'd lost her nerve after her husband left. Her confidence had left, too.

"Mary, that color looks good on you. I really like it." Lillie reached out to feel the fabric.

By the time they reached Bluffton, they were ready for the Seafood Shack Lillie spotted.

"I may have to walk to the movies after that meal." Mary said after the meal and tried to stand taller.

"Actually we could do that. It's not but about four blocks back that way." Sahara had spotted the theater when they had driven around the courthouse circle.

After they passed the local drugstore and candy store they spotted a grand opening sign.

"What's that? I like grand openings. Sometimes they give away stuff." Lillie stepped up to the front window with the others immediately behind.

"A costume shop?" Gloria questioned. She took in all the merchandise in the front window. Too bad, it closed at 5:00." Something nagged at the back of her mind. She'd never cared about costumes.

"Well, maybe next time. Who's up for popcorn?" Sahara was surprised to hear herself.

"A movie's not a movie without popcorn, right?" Gloria was smiling to herself about when her father took her to see "23 Paces to Baker Street" It was a good mystery movie. That was the only kind she mentioned after her mother died. She knew her fatherliked those or the FBI show.

"Hey, we'll have to come back here soon. Look what's playing next.

"Gone with the Wind." Lillie pointed toward the poster display.

"Yeah, that staircase scene, wow!" Mary pledged allegiance with her hand over her heart.

"You know we could do this at least once a month. Have a movie club!?" Sahara was getting in the spirit of things. She felt good being in a group of women. That hadn't happened in a long time.

"You putting that in the form of a motion?" Gloria laughed.

"If that means vote for it, yes. How about it, everybody?"

Sahara looked around the circle.

"Count me in," Lillie spoke up .

"Me, too," Ollie and Mary spoke together.

They walked into "Rear Window" feeling they had made a life-changing decision.

Gloria's mind had drifted to the window of the costume store again then just as quickly to her big car that had transported them to the night out together. It could serve two purposes, now. That would be good for all of us, she thought.

Chapter 75

THE PIT

Five-thirty, Donald thought. What a time to schedule a tour. Was it because it was a personal tour? Oh, well, he supposed 5:30 was the end of the workday. Employees would be going home by then. Usually. The closer he got to the mining pit, though, the louder it got. Truthfully, you needed earplugs to protect your ears from the noise. The grinding of gears, the pounding of drills, the scraping of rock. It was not as loud as downtown New York, but loud enough. They must be working overtime.

Actually he was glad he was going to be viewing from Adam's perspective and explanation. There was way too much that he didn't know about phosphate mining. He'd read a little, basically what they'd given him.

So he could surely learn a thing or two. Was that what he was going to say? That he'd come down here to have a closer look with guide. He hadn't actually been invited, had he? Would that cause problems with Adam? Well, he couldn't worry about that. What was important was Ollie.

He knew there were drills so many feet across. These were placed based on where the ore was and how much "overburden" there was. There were "benches," a lot of these, to mark where drilling had been

190

done and where the ore had been located. The size of the field or open pit related to how to how far out the benches were. Originally, some 30,000 acres had been marked for mining, he remembered. This place must be rich in phosphate. He'd heard only about one mine in 100 was profitable.

He knew there were bucket excavators to collect the ore that had been mined and to take it to the barges. That the barges carried any phosphate that had been "dredged" from the river or dug from the ground down canals to the seaport.

He saw why they needed steel-toed work boots in this place. Hardhats, for sure, and thick hide gloves. As he approached the pit he saw Adam and Ollie at a distance. Adam seemed to be pointing out things and trying to talk to her. Ollie cupped her hand over her ear as if to signal that she couldn't hear him. Why in God's name weren't they wearing hard hats out here?

He would just keep an eye on her from here. That might be the best idea. He watched as Adam pointed toward the barges in the far distance. Ollie shook her head in assent. Then Adam picked up a spade at his feet and jabbed at the ground to show her how hard it was, Donald reckoned. He gestured toward the steam shovels and was probably explaining their use to help get at the ore. He turned back to the barges and was pointing toward the canal which flowed east toward the coast.

A huge noise back of him claimed his attention. It was a bull dozer being driven by someone in a white coat. He squinted to make out the person. Randall, the office manager?

What in the!!! He had the machine at full throttle. It was pointed at Adam and Ollie. God help them! They were right in his path. Why was he headed their direction? Donald broke out running, screaming. The bull dozer rumbled along, bouncing on the uneven parts of the pit. Couldn't Adam hear it coming? Was he the only other person here? Didn't Randall know how to operate it? It he didn't, why in God's name was he driving it? And right at Ollie and Adam. His running pillmill had put him at the back of the machine. He saw it could be suicidal to jump on it but saw no recourse.

Donald threw his body upward onto the dozer's heaving back and clawed his way up toward Randall. Randall was oblivious to him. No, Randall had now just turned and seen him. The expression on Randall's face was murderous. Donald lunged and tried to tackle his arms. He succeeded in grabbing the steering wheel with one hand and swung it sharply left. The huge machine veered violently, teetered precariously, and turned over like a giant dinosaur. That was the last thing Donald felt.

When Adam had heard the roaring behind him and realized a bull-dozer was bearing down on them, he reached for Ollie and tried to throw them both to the side. When he looked up, he knew that it was too close on them. There wasn't time to jump and run. Then he saw someone... Was that Donald? Trying to tackle Randall?! Turning the thing just in time. But then it heaved over on its side and rumbled still, cutting off.

He felt his heart had stopped and heard Ollie scream in recognition of what had happened.

Chapter 76

JUSTICE?

They all sat in the mining office, looking numbly at each other. Billy, Abby, Ollie, and Adam. The company ambulance siren could still be heard in the distance. There was no room for anyone else to ride in the van, according to the emergency team. Going by separate car was the only answer. Adam said he would drive them there. He just had to get his car keys and lock the building. They followed him inside like so many robots and sat down stiffly. No one spoke. Adam pulled his keys from the top desk drawer.

"Let's go, folks, I'll call my wife from the hospital." Adam held the door for the three of them to leave the building. He prayed to himself as he did, God please don't let their son die, too. They all got into the large Lincoln in silence. Adam glanced back at Abby. She was in such shock she looked childlike and lost between Billy and Ollie. Billy still wasn't talking. He just held her small hand in his big one. Adam notice that Ollie's eyes weren't leaving her mother's face.

The drive to the hospital was totally quiet. Adam didn't know what to say to this family. Some people would ask had they done something wrong to have another calamity this close to the other one to go through. He wondered.

As they turned into the emergency entrance, Adam heard Abby who usually made all the pronouncements, ask in a little voice, "Billy, do you think God breaks us in little pieces to make us like he wants us?"

Billy was at loss, though, too. "I wish I knew, Abby,"

Adam felt guilty. If Donald hadn't been on the lot today, he hated to think. Why had he been out there? One thing for sure, if Donald hadn't been out there, he (Adam) would be on that stretcher instead, Donald had saved his and Ollie's lives.

They sat like so many statues in the waiting room. Why hadn't the doctors or somebody have come out and told them something by now? He felt utterly helpless. He realized how little he knew about hospital waiting rooms or emergency rooms. His family didn't live here but most of them were still alive, at least. He surely was going to plan a trip home soon.

He'd heard once that if you didn't know what to say, you could just be with the person. That that could help. He couldn't remember many times in his life when he was speechless before now.

Two doors in the end of the room swung open. One woman and one man, in green scrubs. Were they both doctors?

"We just finished surgery. Are you folks the family?"

"Yes sir." Billy's throat needed clearing.

Abby leaned forward, her hands grasped the chair sides. Ollie's arms were tight beside her body straight down from her shoulders. Her fingers gripped the seat of the sofa.

The man spoke. "I'm Dr. Vance; this young woman is Dr. Singleton. I'm afraid we have some bad news. We tried every procedure we knew to save him. Nothing worked. His body was just too broken from the dozer falling on him."

Billy didn't pause.

"Are you sure? What was his name? There were two men on that dozer. Two men were brought in to you."

At the question the doctor frowned and shook his head. "Robert Randall was theonly one in surgery. You're his family?"

"No, our son, Donald, was on the ambulance, too. We're his family. Where...?"

Dr. Vance's bushy eyebrows raised high when he peered sidelong at his associate over his glasses.

"Dr. Singleton, do you have any idea where the patient named Donald is?"

"How could you lose our son? Abby grabbed Billy's arm and stood up.

"If he isn't getting help already, you need to put out an alarm." Adam stood up.

"I'm alright, just a few bruises. I was knocked out, but the dozer threw me clear."

The voice was unthinkable. And there he was walking up on crutches, his left leg in a cast, a bandage on his forehead.

Abby saw something in Donald's eyes, she thought, for the very first time. She couldn't name it already. But she knew it was good.

Chapter 77

HOSPITAL VISIT

Ollie had gone into the ladies' room off the hospital lobby to wash off any other dirt from the mining field accident. She looked in the mirror over the sink while she scrubbed her hands. It suddenly hit her right between the eyes that she had been the object of Randall's hate. He had wanted to kill her. She stood there drying her hands until she looked down and realized the towel was coming apart from her rubbing. This was new. She had never felt anyone hated her before. She had never given them reason to. This recent stand she had taken on the mine and the water and environment issues had put her in the light. The way Dorrie spoke out on things she didn't like had certainly caused people to dislike her, at least some like the phosphate officials and the people more concerned about money than safety. She opened the door to go out.

She heard a male voice in the waiting room, calling her name, "Ollie, is that you?"

"Are you all right? I was so worried when I heard the emergency whistle go off at the mine! And then I called the ambulance company, and they said that several of your family members were over here at the hospital. I had to come and see about you!"

Ollie had never heard Herb say so many words at one time.

He was wringing his hands. He still had on his apron.

"Hello, Herb. You were so nice to come. Thank you."

He started taking off his apron at her voice.

"Thank God you're alright, Ollie." He rushed forward taking both her hands in his.

"I had to come, I had to come. I was so worried, Thank God you're al...alright!"

It dawned on Ollie that Herb's worry could have pushed him back to when Carly was in the hospital. She reached her arms around his shoulders and hugged him to her.

"It's o.k., Herb." She felt him let out a big breath and a shudder as she held him close. That wasn't all, though. In a moment she felt his arms close around her and his hand pull her cheek against his shoulder. She'd never realized he was so tall.

"Yes, it is," he answered.

Chapter 78

"SUNDAY-GO-TO-MEETING"

O llie couldn't believe it. This was the first Sunday Abby hadn't tried to tell her what to wear to church. She had on a new dress, one the rest of the girls had gone with her to buy. She looked down at her lap, amazed at the colors she'd picked out...coral, purple, and gold...She looked like one of her mother's Iris patches. Smiling to herself, she thought that might be why her mother didn't object. Gloria had told her the brighter colors were quite becoming to her.

Ollie smiled as she looked down the row at Gloria, Lillie, and Sahara. Mary and Travis were sitting together on the other side of Sahara, and all of them returned her smile. Back to Gloria, Lillie, and Sahara sat Donald, Chad, and Chad's fireman friend, in that order.

They had set up their Time Together Club to attend a movie every month. Last month, however, the girls decided to go shopping an extra day and enjoy sharing opinions about what they were buying. They had tried on some pretty outlandish clothes, bought one dress each, and promised each other they would stop together again.

Ollie picked up her church bulletin. It now contained a calendar of the week's events. She saw the listing for the annual summer social for the church. There were new people in the town who should be invited, she thought. Quite a few. The town had really grown since the phosphate mining had begun. First Herb, then…

Galveston interrupted her thoughts.

"I have cut today's sermon, folks, not the main ideas but my elaboration on them."

"Adam and Fulton have informed me that they would like time at the end of the sermon to give us news about the phosphate mining company. Also, Sheriff Roberson has some information about the fire investigation for us. "Not that all of this won't be in the newspaper tomorrow, but he is interested in getting a correction in place today."

"Now, that said, you might not hear today's sermon, although what I have to say may be new and different, as well."

"I see some raised eyebrows. Well, folks, I've done a lot of soul-searching and I find that I stand differently on some issues in the Pentecostal Church. I'm hoping it won't affect my position as your minister, but nonetheless, I must say what I feel."

"We have been too literal, I think, about the business of Paul's admonition to women to be in submission to their husbands. So often, I think, some men have used this scripture out of context as backup for some very abusive behavior. Some women who haven't obeyed their husbands have endured beatings or verbal abuse. I feel sure you would not like the church to be responsible for teaching that behavior. So, I must say let us review the total context of that scripture. It also says in my Bible in Galatians that husbands should honor their wives.

"Also, of secondary importance because I am stating what may be my opinion only, why do we require that our women wear no makeup or combs or ribbon in their hair? We men strut like peacocks, then tell our women, no jewelry and dark, dismal-colored clothes. Now you may say that it says just that in the Bible, but we are now in the 20th century, and I think it is time to review what might be an outdated custom. The church elders may give me my walking papers over this, but I feel I should tell you where I stand on this matter. I believed that women can be expected to use good sense in what they wear to church. I don't expect anyone to wear mini-skirts next Sunday. But to tell them that they are not allowed to wear lipstick or ribbons in their hair seemun necessarily strict and punitive. I'll bet even Eve wore flowers from the Garden in her hair. Do you really think God would have disapproved of that?"

"I'm sure that there'll be call for more discussion on these matters, but for today that's where I stand. Now, I would recognize Sheriff Roberson."

Ollie could hardly believe what she'd just heard, but she was sure the article in the news about the man in the next county convicted of wife-beating had been weighing on Galveston's mind. As far as his ideas on women using lipstick or combs, she was so glad to hear it, she reached for Lillie's hand and squeezed it. Lillie squeezed hers back. Ollie heard Gloria say "I don't believe it" and Mary say "Amen."

The Sheriff held a paper in his hand to which he referred. "I am holding a coroner's report on Briggs here. I am relieved to report to you that there was no wrong-doing on Briggs' part. He suffered a heart attack and collapsed. That was why he failed to cut off the pump after he went to the man's rescue in the car. I know how much many of you thought of Briggs and his serious commitment to his job."

"And Robert Randall...deceased, we found in our investigation, a hat, beard, and suit in the trunk of his car which marks him as the mystery man who feigned a heart attack in front of Briggs at the pump. We now know he was averse to anyone who criticized the phosphate mining industry. His attempt on Dorie's life succeeded, but thankfully his attempt on Ollie's did not due to the heroic efforts of her brother, Donald."

A lot of conversation followed the Sheriff back to his seat.

Fulton walked forward in his stately manner and tapped the pulpit with the gavel to quiet the murmuring.

"Adam has said that since I spoke with you on two previous occasions, I should deliver the current report. We still lack a full record from the water tests and the effect of mining on the animals and ultimately on us who inhabit the community. As soon as that comes to our desks we promise to give you that information. In the interim I would strongly suggest that you boil any water for drinking purposes. All-Green Phosphate, however, has made the decision to construct separate lunchroom facilities on the premises of the company to provide safer working conditions for our employees. Let us know if you would also like lunch prepared for sale to you. Here are forms on which to cast your vote about that." He handed Galveston a stack.

A cheer and several whistles went up in approval.

Fulton help up his hand. "We will also build showers for our employees on site. We will start the building process day after tomorrow and we should expect completion before the 4th of July. Thank you for your attention. I will ask Galveston to return the votes on prepared lunches to me. You might want to thank Olivia and her father Billy Fuller for their intervention in this matter. They were responsible for bringing the special need for this construction to our attention. Those two were not received by Randall very well that day and a day prior. I must apologize for that. I hope they will feel free to contact me in the future with any more questions or issues." Fulton looked directly at Ollie with these closing remarks.

Many members clapped as Fulton returned to the pew he shared with Adam.

Adam nodded in support of Fulton's speech.

Although Ollie had been sidetracked for a moment by the ring of her formal given name; "Olivia" did sound very nice out loud, and she promised herself not to back away from pushing for what her sister Dorrie had started, the ongoing accountability of the phosphate mining company for the environmental protection of this community.

Sweetwater was no longer the jumping off place. This was a meeting place for people, people who benefited from each other's friendship and grew from relationships with one another.

Her mother was playing the closing music. It was "How Firm A Foundation."

'That soul that on Jesus doth lean for repose
I will not, I will not desert to its foes
That soul, though all hell should endeavor to shake
I'll never, no never, no never forsake.'

She stood tall as she stood up. The hymn could be about her, she thought.

After the last majestic sounds of the piano her mother played, she picked up her pocketbook to leave.

Someone laid a gentle hand on her shoulder.

"Would you excuse the apron and do me the great honor of accompanying me to Sunday dinner at The Calla Lily. I closed the restaurant for 15 minutes so I could come down and ask you. Most all your friends will be there. You don't have to go home and cook, do you?"

Ollie was speechless at first. She finally said, "No...I mean, yes."

Herb looked puzzled. "That means you can't or can?" His shoulders drooped.

"No, I don't have to cook, and yes, Herb, I am happy to go eat with you at The Cally Lily!" She grabbed his arm. She noticed his chest swell. And as they walked out of the door into the sunlight, he covered her hand with his and held it tight.

Chapter 79

A NEW VIEW

Yesterday the leaves on the crepe myrtle trees at the back of the house sported dark green hues in the shadow of the setting sun. Now they were brilliant primary green in the midday sun. A black cowbird with a brown head flew like an arrow from his perch and resembled a starling in this light. He attacked two red blooming begonias she had hung in pots from a trellis, breaking two stalks with blooms that fell to the ground. Ollie scrambled from her chair in the Mimosa's shade like a hawk ready to descend on its prey.

"You better get out of my begonias," she clapped he hands to scare him off.

"They're to bloom for us to look at, not for you to sit on. You go get those bread crumbs."

The cowbird fussed his different view for a moment, then flew off to a wet, dark corner of dirt to search for a worm.

"You can disagree with me all you want. That's o.k. Just don't bother my begonias.

"Talking to yourself again, sis?" Donald rounded the corner, grinning at her.

"No, to the birds… Do you know about the cowbird, Donald?"

"Can't say that I do, Ollie, but you're going to tell me, aren't you?"

"Well, the bird book says they used to follow the buffalo and didn't make nests. They just used other birds' nests to lay their eggs in. The other bird would hatch the cowbird's egg along with her own. She never knew any difference."

"Mmm, she wouldn't be well thought of, would she?" Donald mused.

"Who knows? It takes all kinds, I reckon, to make a family."

Donald got quiet.

"Hey, look who's here." Billy had just walked out the back door onto the screened porch.

"Hey Mom, Dad, ya'll got any leftovers for lunch?" He squinted his eyes against the bright sun.

"Now that's an honest question;" Abby laughed, "a lot of people don't fancy leftovers.

"Then they haven't had your cooking, Mom."

"Don't say too much; it might give her a swelled head, son." Billy said this and hurried away from her making a swat at his backside.

"When you think those two will grow up. Donald?" Ollie stood from her chair.

"I hope never, sis." Nobody saw him wipe his eyes when he walked last into the house.

Postscript

This piece of fiction started out to be about a horrific fire and a wonderful woman who died in it, seen by her mother as her "brightest and best" It is also concerned with her younger, less-favored sister, her family, and her community who are left behind to deal with the loss. As I revisited this little town which was part of my past, the story did what they say often happens once the author start it; it took on a life of its own. Other characters were born and interacted, and an extremely important environmental issue raised its head.

The issue of phosphate mining and its after effects loom large, and they are as yet unresolved over forty years after the time setting in this book. If they say there are no dangers resulting from the mining, they may be focused only on the positive gains such as growth of larger economic bases for poorer areas, fertilizers for the world market, strata of the mining fields for study by archeologists, and the American Dental Society's premise that fluoride, a product of phosphate mining, prevents cavities.

I wonder, however, how they can ignore the wastelands left behind after unrestricted phosphate mining, the drying up of essential wetlands, the destruction of some fifty percent of the fish in many of the rivers and streams formerly abundant with them. Why have suits been filed against the federal government and two mining companies by three environmental groups in Idaho for violating the Clean Water Act (2003) for loss of farm animals and burning of crops by radioactive chemicals in the air produced by nearby mines? These groups claim inadequate regulation of phosphate mining in Eastern Idaho is responsible for excessive levels of selenium, which has killed sheep and horses and prompted a warning against eating fish from a local creek. Why has the Canadian Broadcasting Corporation called the phosphate industry a "Pandora's Box"? "That while it brought wealth to rural communities, it also brought ecological devastation? What about the dropping of tons of hazardous waste into the Florida aquifer by overflow from the huge abandoned gypsum stacks (1994) and the attempt to correct that problem by emptying tanks of the waste into the Gulf of Mexico? (2004) Will radioactive gypsum, another product of phosphate mining be added to roads as a cheaper paver since lime rock is beginning to give out?

"German and Austrian scientists knew in the early 1930s that an overactive thyroid (hyperthyroidism) could be successfully treated by bathing patients in water containing minute amounts of fluoride. They had discovered nearly a century ago that fluoride blocked thyroid function" (Sparrow dancer, 2011)

"Deliberately damaging the thyroid will produce a plethora of symptoms affecting the entire human body from head to toe. Symptoms of thyroid damage and fluoride poisoning include weight gain, edema, kidney disease, kidney failure, hair loss, depression, aggression, aches, pains, skin problems, bone deformities (likely including "arthritis" and spontaneous fractures), sexual/erectile dysfunction, memory loss, weakness, fatigue, heart disease, irritability, cancer, digestive disorders including severe Gerd as a result of swallowing fluoride, nausea, vomiting, visual problems, gum disease, "high cholesterol," connective tissue damage, brittle teeth, dehydration." (Sparrow dancer, 2011)

Two recent studies report a relationship between water treated with silicon fluorides and elevated levels of leads in children's blood (Masters and Coplan 1999, 2000) and a concession form the EPA that despite 50 years of water fluoridation, the EPA has no chloric health studies on silicon-fluorides. Thirty-six studies have found a correlation between fluoride and lower IQ, another reason to be concerned about the effect on children. But 2019 this figure has now increased to 53 studies that support this same correlation.

In 1999, Alcoa Aluminum sent out a memo to its workforce across the globe advising them to have medical checks for lung and bladder cancer due to the fluoride exposure in the aluminum industry. Increase incidence between 1994 and 2000 of mutagenic damage in humans was believed to be caused by fluoride exposure related to increased evidence of fluoride in air and water.

Fluoride is found many more places than water. It is found in dental products, processed beverages and foods such as sodas, juices, sports drinks, beers, and many other processed foods, including infant foods. It is found in grape products, dried fruits and beans, cocoa powders, walnuts, tea, drinks pharmaceuticals. It is also found in mechanically deboned meat, especially chicken fingers and nuggets due to contamination from bone particles.

Dr. William Hirzy of the Environmental Protection Agency said once that were fluoride to be classified as a "known" or even a "probable" carcinogen, then the entire policy of water fluoridation at least in the United States would be finished.

"There is also a natural and unavoidable connection between phosphate mining and radioactive material. It is because phosphate and uranium were laid down at the same time in the same place by the same geological processes millions of years ago. They go together. Mine phosphate; you get uranium."

"If market price improves, 4 US phosphate plants in Louisiana and two in Florida would have the capacity to produce a combined 2.75 million pounds of uranium per year, according to the Department of Energy.

DOE has termed these 4 facilities "Non-conventional Uranium Plants."

What about the workers at these plants and the evidence of usually high cancer rate among them?

What has happened to all the testing that should have occurred, given the preponderance of all this damaging information? Did Greed, Money, or Power put on the brakes?

One hundred, thirty-eight communities, world-wide, have ceased fluoridating their water to date Ninety-seven % of Western Europe has rejected water fluoridation

The Department Of Energy has termed these 4 facilities "Non-conventional Uranium Plants."

What about the workers at these plants and the evidence of unusually high cancer rates among them?

What happened to all the testing that should have occurred, testing that should have preceded the fluoridation of water anywhere before 1950, when it happened?

In 2017 a Fluoride lawsuit was filed. The Center for Disease Control made several admissions during the two-week trial.

Fluoride gets into the fetal brain through the placenta. The CDC agreed also that fluoride interferes with the function of the brain. There is no safe dose known. Fluoride is an endocrine disrupter as well CDC recently reported that dental fluoros is out of control. It is a side effect of overexposure to fluoride which can cause discoloration of teeth and make them look at the worst like brown matchsticks, or gold-colored. One doctor in China showed on film what happened to one classroom full of young children and their teeth. It was sad to see. It is now affecting more than 60% of US teens and not just their teeth.

Since 2010, 274 communities have rejected fluoride. Sixty-four studies have linked fluoride with reduced IQ in children. Excessive fluoride exposure can cause osteoarthritis. Fluoride affects many tissues including bones, brain, thyroid, and kidney. In the middle-aged accumulated pains in joints, knees, elbows, and ankles, and shoulders, and ligaments are occurring.

Judge Edward Chen has not rendered his verdict yet in the Fluoride Trial. He has said, after hearing the evidence presented against fluoridating water that there are serious questions he must raise when he renders his decision. Meanwhile, while we wait, Fluoride Action Network is keeping us well informed as well as books like **The Case Against Fluoride** by Michael Connett, PhD,James Beck, MD, PHD, and H. S Micklem, DPhil. and a film, **Crippling Waters.**

www.ingramcontent.com/pod-product-compliance
Lightning Source LLC
Chambersburg PA
CBHW020631110726
47899CB00002B/736